WONDER BREAD AND ECSTASY

WONDER BREAD AND ECSTASY

THE LIFE AND DEATH OF JOEY STEFANO

BY CHARLES ISHERWOOD

ALYSON PUBLICATIONS
LOS ANGELES

Manufactured in the United States of America.
Printed on acid-free paper.

This trade paperback original is published by Alyson Publications Inc.,
P.O. Box 4371, Los Angeles, California 90078.
Distribution in the United Kingdom by Turnaround Publisher Services Ltd.,
Unit 3 Olympia Trading Estate, Coburg Road, Wood Green,
London N22 6TZ, England.

First edition: November 1996

10 9 8 7 6 5 4 3 2

ISBN 1-55583-383-7

Library of Congress Cataloging-in-Publication Data
Isherwood, Charles.
    Wonder bread and ecstasy : the life and death of Joey Stefano / by Charles
Isherwood. — 1st ed.
        ISBN 1-55583-383-7 (pbk)
    1. Stefano, Joey, 1968–1994.   2. Motion picture actors and actresses—United
States—Biography.   3. Erotic films.   I. Title.
PN2287.S6763I84 1996
791.43'028'092—dc20
[B]   96-26524
                                                       CIP

Credits
    From "The Ups and Downs of a Porn Star: Joey Stefano" by Sabin from *Gay
Video Guide,* Volume 1, Number 1. © 1991 by Sabin. Reprinted by permission.
    From "Secrets of the Porn Stars" by Dave Kinnick from *Advocate Classifieds,*
Issue 37, February 22, 1994. © 1994 by Dave Kinnick. Reprinted by permission.

*"All excellence has a right
to be recorded."*

—Dr. Johnson

PROLOGUE

The teaser told the whole story. Over a photo of the spectacularly blond porn starlet Savannah, an announcer intoned, "Is the sex industry to blame for the deaths of these two young stars? Find out what their friends say next, exclusively on *The Marilyn Kagan Show*!" There was just the vaguest breath of a question mark at the end of the first phrase. As the image of Savannah faded from the TV screen, it was replaced by that of a beautiful young man with clear green eyes and a broad, disarming smile, the kind all too rarely found in the movies that had made his name, Joey Stefano, a well-known one the world over among both connoisseurs and casual consumers of gay porn.

The show was a bonanza for Kagan, an L.A. radio psychotherapist who had parlayed her talent for easygoing earnestness into a daily talk show on Los Angeles's Channel 9. It was the height of talk TV's hegemony, before politicians began bashing it and the backlash began, sweeping off the national airwaves a horde of hosts—including Kagan herself, temporarily—as peremptorily as they had been swept on. Today's topic was something of a triple play: In addition to the sufficiently lurid matters of sex and death, it had the added bonus of a drag queen, in the spectacular person of Chi Chi LaRue, the gay porn auteur who was both a friend of Savannah's and the man who had helped shape Stefano's career and directed many of his movies.

He sat on the Kagan couch in a pink faux fur jacket over something in black net that didn't begin to conceal his considerable girth, his white-blond wig tastefully teased, subtle plum lipstick applied to perfection. Flanking him were Savannah's "manager and confidante," Nancy, and Sharon Kane, a leonine beauty in a shoulder-baring black top who was described as an adult-film star and "lover" of Stefano's. A good six feet of temporarily guestless couch stretched in both directions.

A taped video with breathless voice-over detailed the grim facts. Savannah, at age 23, had put a gun to her head in her garage in the hysterical aftermath of a car accident in July 1994, while Stefano had died of a drug overdose at Cedars-Sinai Medical Center after being found unconscious at the suitably seedy Hollywood La Brea Motel the following November, his 26-year-old body shot through with a lethal cocktail of assorted drugs.

The host, a benign-looking, slightly zaftig woman with a sweet face and sensible Sally Jessy eyeglasses, gets right to the point: "So who's to blame for these tragic deaths?" she asks with mildly perky earnestness. The first tragic death to be accounted for, after the first commercial break, is Savannah's, to be sure, probably because she was a star of straight films and her life was more deeply tinctured in celebrity, as

Polaroids flashed on the screen of Savannah with Marky Mark and Pauly Shore duly attest. But her manager-confidante proves telegenically deficient—kind and touching, perhaps, but no match for a drag queen in fake fur. And Savannah's father, "who happens to be on the phone with us," as Kagan put it, happened to hang up sometime during a commercial break. So Kagan steers the show briefly to tragic death number two.

When LaRue and his fellow panelists aver that Stefano had been haunted by a host of problems before he even got involved in the adult-film industry, Kagan zeroes in: "But let me interrupt you: Isn't it true, though, with so many statistics I read, that when kids—runaways—get into porn, they're already screwed up and that the industry screws them up some more?" LaRue bristles a little; maybe in the past, he acknowledges, but things are different in the '90s. He smoothly works in a bid for gay porn as public interest: "We make the movies so you can stay home and whack yourself...you know." Whether the studio audience buys the logic or not, this first bit of ribaldry seems to wake them from their torpor; they give a sniggering round of applause. But they're not on the drag queen's side for long. With the sleeping dragon finally awake, the talk-show dynamic of orchestrated antagonism begins to kick in.

"Is there a connection between drugs, porn, and suicide?" Kagan muses, rather disingenuously, since the point of the show is to capitalize on the lurid stew of these elements, pithily summed up in the colorful logo SEX DRUGS & VIDEOTAPE that pops up on the screen every few minutes to entice channel surfers.

In the brief minutes during which the details of Stefano's sad odyssey are being discussed, LaRue and Kane point out that, in fact, no one knows if he was seeking to end his life when he set out on a binge that might have been expected to end like many another of his binges: with a long, tortured sleep and a gradual return to the surface. But Kagan is not convinced: "Well, you know, he was shooting up and having a lot of problems with drugs..." The dragon threatens to nod off again as Kagan delves for some dirt that might support the suicide thesis, which is infinitely better-suited to daytime television than the idea of an accidental overdose. LaRue and Kane talk about the vagaries of careers in the industry, about Stefano's speedy rise to the top of the gay-porn pantheon and the pressures that entailed, and about the ephemeral nature of all careers forged in porn, where new faces—and more pertinent parts of the anatomy—supplant the old in quick succession. And then LaRue mentions that Stefano's HIV diagnosis may have preyed on his mind.

This is music to Kagan's ears. "So maybe it *was* about suicide!" She turns briefly to Kane. "Had he talked to you about that? And—wait a minute! HIV-positive, and he was still having sex in movies!" This is a potential gold mine of shock value, and Kagan had almost let it pass unexplored. When LaRue gives a frank answer in the affirmative, the audience groans its outrage.

"So this was a guy who not only wanted to hurt himself but wanted to hurt others..." Kagan continues, keeping the scandal momentum firmly on track. LaRue demurs, saying emphatically, "That's not true. We have safe sex in the industry." But the audience is having none of this; it jeers at the mention of safe sex and porn in the same breath.

Kagan, meanwhile, is back on the drug track, and the names Savannah and Stefano more or less disappear from the discourse for the remainder of the show, which grows increasingly circuslike as more guest panelists crowd the Kagan couch. Joining the panel are porn performers Dominique Simone and Bill Marlowe. Simone, a pretty, sensitive-looking black woman, gets the first question. "Dominique, we're talking about drugs and suicide and the death of young people," Kagan says informatively, as if they might just as easily have been talking about political turmoil in Kazakhstan. "Are there a lot of drugs in the industry?"

Simone contends that they are just as prevalent in the mainstream entertainment industry. "Me, myself, I never saw drugs on the set," she says.

Kagan takes another tack. "Can I ask a question that isn't anywhere, that just comes to my head: Do you think that there's more pain and suffering with people who go into the sex industry than legitimate theater or mainstream movies?"

"The entertainment industry—period—is very stressful," says Simone rather wanly.

Kagan cuts in quickly. "I'm sorry. I have to say it: the entertainment industry versus porn. It's a different kind of person who goes in there," she says flatly, throwing a not-so-veiled insult in the face of her panelists.

This cruel cue is picked up by a mild-mannered young blond man in the audience who stands up and addresses a question to "the individual in pink."

"You mentioned that stability is necessary to be in the industry," he says (though it was Marlowe and not LaRue who had made the point). "Do you consider yourself to be emotionally and psychologically stable?"

The sneer is clear, but LaRue holds his own. "If I wasn't, I wouldn't dress like this," he laughs. The audience applauds; score one more for the drag queen.

The next interlocutor is a young man in *Reservoir Dogs* drag: black suit, white shirt, black shades. He doesn't mince words. Peering presumably at LaRue, he starts off in high dudgeon: "I wonder how you could be such a hypocrite when you could snort the paint off the walls, you do so much coke!"

5

This sends the audience into a pleasurable titter. "With you, honey," LaRue shouts back. "With you, Jeff Stryker!"

Kagan turns quizzically to her special guest antagonist, asking him to introduce himself.

"I'm Jeff Stryker," he says, and there is a slight pause, perhaps for applause that doesn't come; the audience is clearly unaware of the size of his mail-order business, not to mention the size of his genitalia.

"You're a part of the porn industry, a porn superstar," Kagan supplies.

He murmurs modestly before planting his standard in a gruff, nervous shout. "I'm here because this hypocrite puts people with AIDS with people that don't."

The name of Stefano surfaces briefly as Stryker accuses LaRue of planning to make a film pairing the HIV-positive porn star with other porn models without informing them of the risk; this gets a riot of howls from the audience, who seem to smell blood.

LaRue and Stryker squabble for a while about safe sex in the industry, with Stryker calling LaRue "little queeny" and LaRue countering, "That's *big* queeny, Jeff." Joining the fray is actor-director Gino Colbert, also attired in a dark suit and shades, who implicitly accuses LaRue of supporting performers' drug habits. The audience boos cheerfully; they seem willing to watch this fight forever.

But the couch has not yet reached capacity, so after the next commercial break we meet three more veterans of the biz: starlet-turned-producer Tyffany Million and performers Ryan Block and Jamoo. Ms. Million takes charge. A smart blond who fights the audience's contempt with an ample supply of her own, she answers Kagan's umpteenth drug-use question with a firm "I've never seen it on any set I've worked on."

Wrong answer, Tyffany; the crowd boos. She follows up with an explanation: The business is becoming more acceptable, less sleazy; drugs are frowned upon. No one seems to be listening.

On to Jamoo, who says, "I haven't seen it on a set, but I'm going to have to disagree. There is use..." This gets an immediate round of applause. But it's clear to anyone paying attention that they're not applauding his honesty; they're applauding his saying what the audience wants to hear.

Tyffany counters that drug use isn't particularly unusual in any sector of society, and Marlowe contends that he never got drugs from anyone in the industry, but Kagan knows her audience and presses the right buttons. "But there's a concept still—and maybe it's wrong. People say the porno business is predicated on new young flesh that comes in from somewhere else, and they use drugs as, like, a lure!"

The audience doesn't wait for anyone to answer; this idea is too familiar, too comfortable to risk contradiction, so they go ahead and applaud the contention, and all attestations to the contrary are jeered down as the show lumbers to a close.

The deaths of Savannah and Stefano, "tragic" or otherwise, were the ostensible subject of the show, but there was little illumination thrown on the causes of their ends. Was it a moment of sudden despair that made nothingness more attractive to Savannah than a trip to the hospital? Was Stefano's fatal cocktail a grim inevitability after a life of living on the edge or an act of sudden self-destruction? The show didn't supply any answers or even a forum to search for them. No matter how sensational their demises, after all, dead people can't go on talk shows and either receive or inflict insults.

But there may have been a clue to the mysteries left behind by Savannah's and Stefano's deaths in the simple dynamics of the show, whose unpleasant tenor illustrated clearly the facile contempt the public has for the adult-film industry. In the American mind, sex and money—those two cornerstones of human existence—aren't supposed to be connected. Whether idealism or Puritanism is at its root, Americans like to believe that sex is the one area where capitalism should not rear its lovely head. So people who make a living off sex—and, to a degree, their employers and customers—are reserved for special contempt; hence the spectacular media coverage that attended the stories of Heidi Fleiss and Hugh Grant. And hence the barely concealed disgust that animated the Kagan studio audience.

Whatever the private griefs they juggle, the mixture of hurts and happinesses their lives contain, the young men and women who pursue careers in porn are chasing the American dream across a chasm of contempt, sometimes from family and friends they look to for support. The pleasure they give people is easy to trivialize; and as the *Marilyn Kagan* circus so vividly indicated, so are their lives.

CHAPTER ONE

As befits a legendary beauty, the early days of Joey Stefano are somewhat shrouded in obscurity. He liked to keep it that way, from a combination of factors that seemed to be dominated by a general air of bad memories, of an unhappy youth best left unremembered and undetailed. It is known that he was born Nicholas Anthony Iacona Jr. on New Year's Day, 1968. That's an almost too-interesting date: The first day of a year that would go down in American history as one of almost unprecedented unrest. It's tempting to stretch for symbolic meaning where hard facts leave a void. And, indeed, there's something appropriate about the man who would be Joey Stefano being born on the crest of a social revolution. He would never live by the rules of his parents' generation and would make a career of flouting middle-class proprieties, which were, after all, what revelers during the summer of love were aiming at. Some twenty years later, when most of those who had tuned in, turned on, and dropped out were tuning up BMWs, turning on CNN, and dropping in to the best restaurants, Nick Iacona would be following flamboyantly in the traditions they had forsaken: turning on to the kinds of drugs they'd never dreamed of and taking the sexual revolution to new heights, despite the countervailing attitudes that had dominated his youth in the Reagan '80s.

But he wasn't born of a momentary pairing in between student demonstrations. His parents, Helen and Nicholas Sr., were solidly middle-class inhabitants of Chester, Pennsylvania, which is not to be confused with West Chester—and never is. He had two sisters—one older, Linda, and one younger, Tina—and was raised with them in Chester, attending Claymont High School in nearby Claymont, Delaware, until 1983. That year was clearly a turning point in Nick's life, and for the saddest of reasons. He was fifteen years old that year when his father died. An obituary placed by his family after Nick's death states that he "graduated" from high school in 1983, but it is highly unlikely that Nick, at fifteen, would be graduating. He was not known to be bookish, and it would have required an accelerated schedule to graduate some two or three years before his peers. What is more likely, and is confirmed by stories Nick later told friends, is that he dropped out of high school that year.

Whether it was directly connected with his father's death is unclear, but it's not insignificant that the year he lost his father, Nick Iacona Jr. left the path that most young Americans are expected to adhere to if they want to have a chance at the American dream. It seems that at fifteen Nick gave up on hopes of finding success in the middle-class, model-American fashion. He went looking for another way.

The death of a parent is, of course, a traumatic event in the life of anyone, but it is particularly disturbing to an adolescent, caught in the painful period when he is establishing what will become his self-image as an adult. Suddenly the most powerful role model disappears, leaving a void that can't easily be filled. It's only natural that we look to our parents as our primary source of approval as children and young adults—and indeed throughout life; they brought us into the world, and their opinion is at the very bedrock of our self-esteem. When he lost his father, Nick Iacona Jr. lost an important source of validation. In later life he would speak to friends about a sadness stemming from the knowledge that he could never live up to his father's expectations, his father's hopes for him. (He didn't say specifically what those hopes were, but it is interesting that he carried his father's name; that seems to imply a deeper than normal emotional investment on the part of his father in the fortunes of his son—and thus a greater obligation on the part of the son to live up to expectations. Another coincidence that may have served to heighten his sense of a family responsibility is that, according to an interview he gave later, both his father and grandfather were also born on New Year's Day.) And he would never have a chance to objectively examine those feelings of falling short of his father's hopes, because his father was gone. He was left with a profound feeling of inadequacy and no power to fight its cause.

His knowledge of his homosexuality made his father's death even more significant. Gay men's relationships with their fathers are traditionally difficult ones. In his 1989 book *Being Homosexual: Gay Men and Their Development,* psychiatrist Richard A. Isay posits the father-son relationship as the key one in gay men's lives: "Like all forms of love, homosexuality remains mysterious and eludes our total understanding. Like all forms of love, it is a longing for a lost attachment. That longing, for gay men, is usually for the father." The difficulties gay male adolescents face in coming to terms with their sexuality are often centrally symbolized by a strained or antagonistic relationship with a father caused by the suspicion that the father will be—or is—disappointed in the knowledge of the son's homosexuality. "Particular to the childhood of homosexual boys," Isay writes, "is that their fathers often become detached or hostile during the child's early years, as a result of the child's homosexuality. Fathers usually perceive such a child as being 'different' from other boys in the family, from themselves, or from their son's peers.... This may lead to the father's withdrawal.... The withdrawal of the father, which is invariably experienced as a rejection, may be a cause of the poor self-esteem and of the sense of inadequacy felt by some gay men. It is also an important reason why some gay men have difficulty forming loving and trusting rather than angry and spiteful relationships." Of course, much of the hurt can be healed over time if the father comes to terms with his son's sexuality, but for Nick, that was never an option—his father died before the process could continue.

There may have been yet another complicating factor in Nick Iacona's relationship with his father: abuse. He spoke to friends and others of being sexually abused as a child, though the references were few and maddeningly elliptical. Talking to the *Gay Video Guide* in 1991, he spoke about wanting to write a book that would include "my whole story: the sexual abuse, coming out of the closet, the porno, the drugs, everything." An article written after his death for *Manshots* magazine by his friend Mickey Skee explored the muddled stew of his relationship with his father in a brief paragraph: "He said he was never able to hug his father. He told close friends that the man he was named after had molested him as a child and that it was 'no big deal'—something that his older sister, Linda, strongly denies [that denial presumably refers to the molestation, not to its being 'no big deal']—and yet, just before he died, he told close friends that he wanted to be buried with his father."

At the age of fifteen, then, Nick Iacona was left fatherless—in a way, he was faced with the daunting prospect of becoming his father. With Nicholas A. Iacona Sr. gone, Nicholas A. Iacona Jr. was the man of the house. The responsibility—whether it was imagined or intimated—was clearly too much for Nick. Rather than shoulder the burden or make some attempt to, he rebelled. He left school and, apparently, home as well. In an interview for *Thrust* magazine, he gave a grim précis of his youth: "I was sexually molested, and to make a long story short, I moved out on my own. My father died, and I moved out. I did a lot of drugs. I believe I grew up too fast. I had to."

He referred in later years to stints working in a hardware store and for a moving company. But before long he discovered that he had more significant tools he could put to use: his beauty and his sexuality. How he came to start hustling is not recorded, but hustle he did, both on the street and for "escort" services. Before long it became a necessity, as standard jobs would not support his increasing drug habit. He made no secret in later life of his early dependence on drugs, though accounts vary of when he started and what drugs he used. "He told me he had been a heroin addict since he was fourteen and that he worked as a hustler on the street," says Chi Chi LaRue, a friend and associate from 1989. "He'd had a rough life; he didn't want to talk about his home life." Other friends remember stories of angel dust (PCP) and cocaine use, all beginning in his mid teens, around the time of his father's death. Skee's *Manshots* article says, "He ran away from home at sixteen, fleeing to Manhattan, where he turned tricks for food—and

drugs." Eventually, at any rate, he entered a drug-rehab program in Philadelphia with a friend from high school, and for
a significant period of time—up to three years, according to
one account—before moving to California, he was drug-free.

Also mysterious is how Iacona came to be an expert in the
field of gay pornography. He would impress his soon-to-be-
peers in the porn industry with an encyclopedic knowledge of
the names of gay and straight adult-film stars as well as an
uncanny ability to name a player simply by glancing at an
anatomical close-up. It's not likely that he had access to a
family VCR, so his knowledge must have been gleaned from
theaters or the video libraries of friends and tricks. Eventually his fascination with porn, and his hustling work, led him to
see in the video industry a way to escape the confines of his
working-class background. Giving the lie to the popular myth
that porn stars are snatched from respectable life at a desperate point by corrupters with video cameras, Nick Iacona
actively sought an entrée in the business; it was one of the few
decisive acts in his life.

Tony Davis was dancing at Manhattan's Jock Theater when
he was handed a note from what he assumed was an admirer.
Admirers were the whole point of dancing—stripping, more
precisely—at such theaters, which served as advertising
venues for porn stars' personal services. Davis, with his trademark two-tone blond-on-brown hair and immaculately tanned
body, was a veteran in 1989, to put it mildly. He claimed in
1988 to have appeared in nearly a hundred videos, an astonishing figure even by porn standards, where a busy actor can
log a dozen or more videos in a year. The note turned out to
be from Nick Iacona, who appeared at the theater the next
day, revealing himself to be rather different from the usual
Jock Theater customer. At twenty-one, five feet eleven inches

tall, and a more or less ideal 165 pounds, Nick Iacona had the kind of dark good looks that had already made him a noticeable presence on the Philadelphia gay bar scene. His brown hair was on the long side, and he wore a mustache and a wisp of a beard.

He came quickly to the point, telling Davis he was interested in breaking into the business. He said he had already done some hustling and wanted to know if Davis could help him with contacts; he was clearly familiar with the product. Davis took a liking to Iacona and was happy to help. He took some Polaroids of him in his dressing room, the Polaroid shot being the closest thing to a screen test the industry has. Davis could see that if Iacona was as able as he was willing, there was no question that he would be welcomed into the industry. Iacona himself told a somewhat confused version of his entry into the business to *Thrust* magazine later that year: "I wanted to try to get in a magazine, and I didn't know how to go about doing it. I went to a place called [the Jock Theater], and I was cruising the bookstore, and there was this stage downstairs. I was looking at this guy. And, to make a long story short—well, I never went into one of these places where, you know, you pay to watch someone jack off or something like that.

"So I went to pay to watch one of these porn stars [Tony Davis]. I never heard of him before, because my porn star favorites are older guys from way back. I wound up talking to him, and he took my pictures and said he'd see what he could do because he knew some people. I called him a week later and bugged the shit out of him. He told me to come on out [to Los Angeles]."

So Nick Iacona took a plane to Los Angeles and checked in to the Saharan Motor Hotel on Sunset Boulevard, just west of La Brea Avenue, a Hollywood neighborhood whose mild seediness would not have fazed a young man of twenty-one who had spent time prostituting himself in worse locales. He had made the connection he needed.

Davis later gave his impression of Nick Iacona's fundamental motivation in entering the adult-film industry: "He didn't want to do it for the money—he said he wanted to do it for the attention."

The desire for attention is a fairly fundamental one. To need the kind of attention only fame can bring bespeaks an inability to find fulfillment in the attention people get through interpersonal relationships. There was a lack in Nick Iacona's life that he sought to fill by entering the pornography business, by becoming the object of desire of thousands of men. There is no knowing the roots of that ambition, really; Nick Iacona was never a cerebral person and may not have understood it himself. But surely it's not too speculative to propose that in courting the attention of a world of gay men, he was seeking to replace the one man whose attention he could no longer hope to gain: his father's.

CHAPTER TWO

While Nick Iacona was struggling through a difficult youth in Philadelphia, the man who would change the course of his life was growing up in vastly different circumstances in the small town of Hibbing, Minnesota. Larry Paciotti was born in 1959, some nine years before Iacona, to a father who worked as a railroad engineer and a mother who worked in a clothing store. He finished high school in 1978 and even logged a year or two of community college before setting off on a less bourgeois route that would land him at the pinnacle of the gay porn business. Growing up an overweight child who deflected the cruelties of other kids by becoming the class clown, he nurtured a strong interest in pornography almost as soon as puberty kicked in.

The Strand Theater on Minneapolis's Lake Street (now a 99¢ store, Paciotti informs) was the area's primary porn venue, and Paciotti made it a mecca. Like a stagestruck boy in

Manhattan haunting the Broadway houses, Paciotti saw as much as he could; he still remembers the title of the first porn film he saw, at 16—*Pretty Peaches*—and speaks with awe-tinged amusement of the fact that that film was the screen debut of actress Sharon Kane, now among his closest friends.

"I watched the movies in a different way," he remembers. "I didn't go in and jerk off; I'd watch it like I was watching *All About Eve*; I'd take my friends, who would be horrified, and when Samantha Fox would come on with a new hairdo, I'd notice and comment on it. I probably have an obsession with sex and also an obsession with stars. For me, wanting to see the next Samantha Fox movie was like someone wanting to see the next Elvis movie."

The dim recesses of an adult movie theater were an odd place to find comfort, but Paciotti had done battle with the twin burdens of growing up gay and growing up overweight and so was used to feeling an outsider. In small-town America, it's not OK to be gay, it's not OK to be fat, and adult movie houses are naturally forbidden places; chronically overweight and already growing aware of his attraction to men, Paciotti was used to transgressing social taboos, was growing comfortable being an outsider. For a suburban Minnesota boy, there was nowhere more "outside" than a porn theater. And although there was no gay porn theater in the city, at the straight porn theater Paciotti could seek surreptitious satisfaction of his homosexual attraction by viewing the gay reels that ran in some of the private coin booths, while Amber Lynn gyrated on the big screen.

But his odd hobby would remain just that for several years, as he did time—eight years, in fact—in a pizza joint when he left Hibbing for the biggest nearby city, Minneapolis, to join the ranks of idly artistic homosexuals enrolled in beauty school. Even his keen appreciation of the evolution of porn starlets' tresses wasn't enough to maintain a professional interest in hairdressing. "I went through school and decided I hated it," he says. "It was too subservient. I wanted to be the one in the chair, giving orders."

Although he had been aware of an attraction to boys since puberty and had moved to Minneapolis with a friend he suspected was also gay, Paciotti wasn't open about his sexuality. His sexual adventuring was limited to a clandestinely purchased *Spur* magazine, quickly hidden in his closet, and the coin reels at the straight porn house. "I'd go out to the straight bars with my friends, get drunk, and then stumble down the street to the gay bar, saying, 'I'll be right back,'" he laughs.

He came to terms with his sexuality rather spectacularly, going from closeted pizza-parlor employee to drag queen in a startlingly short period of time. In the early '80s, drag was still the revered but rather hoary institution that it had been for some decades. In gay venues all over America, "female impersonators" aped Barbra or Bette or Joan with wildly varying degrees of success; the other option was the generic disco diva, big-wigged and besequined, lip-synching to tinned music made famous by the black woman of one's choice. But the landscape was beginning to change; from England came singer Boy George, mixing the mechanics of drag with contemporary styles to create an image of indeterminate gender and one that the American public would find sufficiently intriguing—or confusing—to allow the sweet pop of his band, Culture Club, to find remarkable success. When Boy George accepted the band's Grammy for Best New Artist in 1983 with the words "Thanks, America, you know a good drag queen when you see one," it was without a doubt the first time the term had fallen on millions of ears. Also forging new ground on American soil were Divine and John Waters, whose first film collaboration, *Mondo Trasho,* appeared in 1970. It was followed by a series of cult comedies that gradually gained the attention of more adventurous moviegoers and made Divine a household name among the country's more unconventional households.

Of course, Divine was a particular inspiration to Paciotti. The drag-queen ideal had previously been to approximate the contours of presumed female perfection: tall (no problem for Paciotti), buxom (purchasable), and svelte (rather a difficulty). Divine, who was the most famous drag queen of them all (by virtue of his being a movie star), rewrote the rules. Paciotti had been hanging out at Minneapolis's hippest club, First Avenue, for a while. It was the chief watering hole for music mavens— Prince was a regular, as was Joan Jett—and Paciotti, a self-described "rock 'n' roll heavy metal disco funk slut," was regularly in attendance. The club hosted an impersonation contest called the Great Pretenders, and, on a lark, Paciotti and a trio of friends decided to do the Weather Girls in the grand old-school drag tradition. Despite their obvious inexperience— they slapped pancake makeup on over mustaches—they won the contest, receiving $50, which, to a pizza-parlor employee in Minneapolis, was a considerable sum.

Paciotti's drag name came by chance; the quartet began entering the contest every week, winning regularly. But a drag queen without a name is merely a man in a dress. Someone suggested—with a notable lack of novelty—the surname LaRue; Chi Chi had been a nickname Paciotti's dramatic manner had earned him some time earlier. And so was born Chi Chi LaRue.

Paciotti moved to Los Angeles in 1987, answering the call of ambition and escaping the constriction of life in the Midwest. He had dumped the "hag drag" act for a more glamorous— and remunerative—look: "The pretty ones were getting all the cock, and I wasn't." Indeed, although he loved to perform, his most primal motivation for pursuing his drag persona may have been the need for sexual attention; an overweight man is not a cynosure in a gay bar, but when Paciotti got tarted up in drag, he ceased to be just an overweight man and became something entirely different and more alluring. "I got sex when I was in drag," he says flatly, "and I needed that kind of boost to my self-esteem."

With a fellow Weather Girl impersonator in tow, Paciotti found his way to the low-rent nexus of the L.A. drag scene, a gloriously dingy bar on Santa Monica Boulevard called the Four Star. This was no glitz palace: Cockroaches crawled along the mirrors; an old, bitter woman waited tables; and drag queens, from street hookers to showgirls and their admirers, gathered to let down—or put up—their hair. There, LaRue braved the drag-queen initiation rites—the contest—and duly took home the $50 that was apparently the ordained prize for drag contests worldwide. Hosting the contest was one Gender, who'd inherited the mantle when the previous emcee was run out of town, as was occasionally the case with drag queens of the older generation, who lived more precarious existences than the up-and-comers dogging their high heels.

Gender was an original, a mix of Anita Ekberg and Donna Reed, whose theatrical training (logged by his male alter ego, born and raised in Downey, California—"home of the Carpenters!") gave him the discipline and dedication to make his performances an expert display of a new camp sensibility. While other Four Star regulars lip-synched to a number and then trawled for tips, Gender sang live, creating his own mini-musical extravaganzas and attempting to ignore the flock of somewhat seedy regulars the bar attracted.

He and LaRue became friendly; they drank together, dressed together, dished together. And as LaRue began to work his way into the gay porn industry, he would call on Gender to bring along his makeup brushes and sure sense of style.

Indeed, it hadn't taken long for LaRue to gain a foothold in the business that had captured his attention at age sixteen. After just a month in L.A., he had found himself with rapidly dwindling cash reserves and no prospects of a job; although he harbored vague aspirations of breaking into gay porn—he'd worked in an adult bookstore for a while before moving to L.A.—he wasn't quite sure how to go about it. But the saint that watches over drag queens—there are a number of likely candidates—was keeping an eye out, and an ad was providentially placed in the paper on the day when LaRue's desperation reached a crisis point and he had to face the inevitability of looking for work. The ad wasn't specific; it stated only that a gay company was looking for a salesman.

When LaRue showed up at the San Fernando Valley offices of Catalina Video, the die was cast. "I knew so much about their product, they hired me immediately," he says. "And I started the next day."

In fact, even an occasional consumer of gay porn would be likely to recognize the Catalina name. Catalina and Falcon were far and away the two largest producers of gay sex videos and had been for years. The founding fathers of the two companies—and their chief directors for many years—were William Higgins at Catalina and Falcon's Chuck Holmes. They had been friends in L.A. in the '70s who turned a casual hobby into rival businesses and by the mid '80s were responsible for the majority of the industry's top-of-the-line productions.

So within weeks of his arrival, LaRue found himself working at the gay porn epicenter, even if his job was a fairly mundane one. "I'd call retailers and say, 'We've got *Powertool* coming out. How many do you want?'" LaRue recalls. He might have been selling bathroom fixtures; in a way, he was.

But the atmosphere was intoxicating for a porn aficionado who had never looked at adult films as a lesser form of film-making. "I met Jeff Stryker, which to me was like meeting Cher," he recalls. "I was shaking."

He was quickly frustrated by his sales position, however, shackled to a phone while young men of nerve-jangling beauty roamed the halls, on their way to who-knew-what constellations of erotic activity. LaRue would shirk his sales chores to file slides of models and gradually badgered his way into the promotion department, a small step closer to the product itself. He was still working the phones, now in order to solicit magazine covers for Catalina's stable of stars, a primary marketing tool for the video companies. He soon got off the phones and onto the photo shoots, art-directing an occasional box cover or magazine layout. But in true showbiz fashion, he found his directing ambitions thwarted by the will of a man in a position of power who did not see the overweight, outspoken LaRue as Catalina directing material.

"He thought I was too big and too loud and too fun and too into everything," LaRue says. In fact, it came down to that first point. "He said I'd never direct unless I lost one hundred pounds—and *he* was a heavy guy!"

It should come as no surprise that an industry that relentlessly promotes physical perfection would find physical imperfection somewhat objectionable even behind the scenes. The porn business, after all, relies on the idea that beauty is a valuable commodity, and the corollary of that notion is that those who lack it are inherently less valuable than those who possess it; that workers in the porn industry should buy into the company line isn't remarkable—what's remarkable is that LaRue and others have succeeded in spite of it. What LaRue's nemesis failed to understand is that making good pornography, like any artistic creation, is essentially an act of the imagination. And it is often those who believe themselves to be the unbeautiful, the undesired, who have lived most fully in their imaginations.

In any case, the opinion that LaRue's career could advance only if he shed a hundred pounds was one not shared by LaRue, and he decided to make a stand. At lunch with *über*-boss Higgins, he bluntly asked to be given a chance to direct, and Higgins agreed. Higgins and LaRue had become friendly. Higgins would drop by the Four Star every Friday to see LaRue perform, spending most of his time playing pinball and the remainder auditioning young men—though they didn't know it. "When he saw a gorgeous guy walking by, he'd say, 'He's cute—go ask him if he wants to do a movie,'" LaRue recalls.

LaRue was given a single dance segment to direct in *Hard Men 2* and had to scramble to pull together a shoot that was, perhaps to make things more difficult for him, scheduled for San Francisco. As he recalls it, everything went fine, but no more assignments followed. The message was clear: LaRue was a great salesman and schmoozer and a lot of fun to have around the office, but he wasn't director material.

So he quit. His armor had always been a bravado that masked profound insecurities, but his instinct that he was born to make porn was now unequivocal. He had made a host of contacts in the industry while working at Catalina and was quickly hired by an upstart company called In-Hand Video. Also located in the Valley, the company was of a considerably lower caliber than Catalina. Budgets were minuscule—running $5,000 or at most $10,000—and videos were shot in a single day. But if the rigors of shooting videos on shoestrings made logistics difficult, they also inspired creativity. And there was no monolithic structure to negotiate, as at Catalina, a company with a major distribution apparatus and one that had perfected a slick product that was expected to be replicated ad infinitum.

At In-Hand there was no house style. LaRue was free to create his own. He cut his teeth on all manner of movies—gay, straight, lesbian, bisexual—and brought to them a sensibility that was a reflection of his drag-queen alter ego. Sometimes it was desperation that fueled the creativity, as on one of his more adventurous sapphic epics, *Lesbos a Go-Go*.

"We shot it in four-and-a-half hours," LaRue recalls, perhaps a record even by low-end-porn standards. "We had rented a space, a nightclub, that we had to be out of by 7 o'clock, and we didn't get started until 3." LaRue and Gender, who was doing makeup and styling, threw their cast of startled porn starlets into some attire that matched the kitsch title. "I pulled all my old camp '60s wigs out of the closet," recalls Gender. "We did these girls like '60s go-go dancers and shot this silly plot. The commercial sex value of the video was nil, but the press touted it, and everyone loved it: lesbians, gay men, straight men."

It was a matter of injecting style into an industry that regularly dispensed with it as a distraction from sex. But for LaRue, style enhanced sex, and his sense of humor was everywhere in evidence. A video called *Itty Bitty Titty Committee* was not likely to sell big numbers, but he was creating an image, a persona, that made a splash in the industry. (That epic, his first lesbian entry, was nominated for an award at the porn industry's trade show.) The idea that a drag queen—an image of gay sensibility at its most feminine—could play a major role in creating the aesthetics of gay porn was an uncomfortable one for some industry veterans. Gender describes their reaction succinctly: "Why should a big fat femme drag queen be telling gorgeous guys how to have sex?" An exalted—and, of course, falsified—machismo is the order of the day in gay porn; the characters who populate gay porn videos aren't florists or hairdressers or interior decorators (as indeed a glance at their video surroundings would indicate). Nor were they drag queens—until Chi Chi LaRue came along.

CHAPTER THREE

Chi Chi LaRue's birthday party took place on a night in November, but porn star Karen Dior (née Geoff Gann) decided to wear a white string bikini anyway. He reasoned that drag queens aren't really dressed appropriately in any event, so they can damn well wear what they please. And the average drag queen isn't likely to find herself in a crowd that objects to white after Labor Day. Dior had met LaRue at the Four Star, naturally, but they had only recently become friendly; it wasn't until the night of the party, in fact, that Gender filled Dior in on the details of LaRue's burgeoning porn career.

Geoff Gann was born in Ozark, Missouri (population: 3,000), the son of one of the town's prominent Republicans, a state senator for most of Gann's life. The state senator's son had cut a rather odd figure in town, forgoing a job in the school library to hawk Mary Kay cosmetics, not an approved pastime for Ozark high school boys. His parents had to stifle their dismay; Geoff was pulling $100 an hour in sales to bored housewives who whiled away the heat of an afternoon being fussed over by the pretty Gann boy. After high school he stayed close to home at his parents' request, attending college in Springfield, but a spring break spent in L.A. brought quickly home the fact that the miseries of gay life in Missouri were not universal. He had meandered from major to major—from music to dance to English to communications—without much enthusiasm, so after finishing a final term he headed west with a friend in August of 1988.

His luggage contained a cosmetology license, which he had picked up in between majors, and a handful of bikinis, his drag trademark. Even in Missouri drag had its place, and Gann had given birth to Karen Dior at a nightclub after setting up house with a college acquaintance who liked to dress in dresses on the side. Gann's name of choice had been Anaïs, a moniker that Missouri girls couldn't quite get their tongues around. "People called me Anus, Anise; nobody could pronounce it," he recalls. "So I picked a name that, no matter how drunk someone is, they can still say it." Hence Karen; *Dior* posed no elocutionary pitfalls either, and it was "a dragqueeny last name."

At LaRue's birthday party, Dior, clad in white bikini, gloves, and heels, presented an image that LaRue found too spectacular not to be captured on video. He proposed that Dior costar in a porn movie he was planning to make with veteran Sharon Kane. *Sharon and Karen* had a certain ring to it, and a drag queen in a skin flick was an untried commodity. There was a small but steady market for videos featuring transsexuals in varying states of transformation, but an anatomically traditional man in bikini and heels was an innovation, and LaRue liked innovation.

Dior, or rather Gann, had some trepidation to quell. "I did the 'Oh, what will my parents think?' for a minute," he recalls. "But I figured tripping around town in a white bikini is a little bit beyond their boundaries anyway, so why not? The people I knew who worked in porn were really nice, and I decided to try it and see if I liked it."

A few weeks later a small crew assembled in producer Paul Pellitieri's studio to shoot the photos that would go on the cover of a box that would contain a video that had yet to be created. Such are the mild perversities of the pornography business. Mainstream films are sold to the public through a barrage of media, from both reviews and advertisements on TV and in newspapers and magazines to word of mouth. Adult movies, on the other hand, have to sell themselves to consumers almost instantaneously. Most consumers of both gay and straight adult films wouldn't know where to find a review if they wanted to, and indeed most of the "reviews" that appear in the gay skin mags are more properly classified as advertorial—they're promotional pieces run in exchange for an ad. Word of mouth is out of the question for all but the most unabashed consumers of porn; many wouldn't even admit to being regular renters of porn videos and aren't likely to give the thumbs-up or thumbs-down during cocktail party conversation. So a video must entice the consumer at the point of purchase, seduce the casual browser from the porn shelf of the video store, where, to make matters more difficult for producers, he may not like to linger indefinitely. Thus does the porn package come to take precedence over the product itself. Sometimes more money is spent producing a polished box cover than is pumped into the actual production of the video; more often than not it's quickly apparent to the consumer, but by then the video is rented—or purchased.

But there was a lot more than the fate of a porn video at stake on the late summer day in 1989 when Chi Chi LaRue, Karen Dior, Sharon Kane, Gender, and photographer Don Mantooth assembled to crank out a box cover—although it's only in retrospect that it can be discerned. LaRue had already begun producing gay videos at a fast clip, but they were largely unspectacular. Mostly made on minuscule budgets for In-Hand, which was notoriously inept at marketing its product, they made a brief stop on video shelves before disappearing into oblivion. His large-as-life persona as a drag queen had gained him the attention of the industry, but the industry didn't know what to make of him; they were amused, but mixed with the amusement was no small share of contempt. LaRue had only a certain amount of time to prove himself to the powers at Catalina, Falcon, and the few other major producers before the spotlight would move on and the drag queen who wanted to be a porn player would be an also-ran.

Sharon Kane too was at something of a crossroads. She had been working in the adult-film industry for an astonishing fifteen years, having begun as a dancer in San Francisco in the '70s working for Alex de Renzi, when the straight film business was centered there. When she met LaRue at a Consumer Electronics Show in Las Vegas in 1987, she had recently started working in the business again after taking time off following several grim years in New York. (At the semiannual CES, which focuses primarily on TV and video technology, adult-film producers and distributors set up booths to flog their wares to retailers. The adult-film arena is segregated from the main convention floor and usually takes place at a different hotel.) LaRue had more or less accosted her as she wandered the floor, enthusing about his appreciation of her work and his desire to work with her. It turned out to be a serendipitous meeting for Kane, who would soon start working heavily in the L.A. straight scene and would soon after that, as she says, "peak." How does an adult-film performer know when she's peaked? "You know you've hit your peak because nobody hires you anymore," she says wryly. Fortunately, when offers for straight movies began drying up, LaRue started to call, hiring Kane for the more polysexual videos he was cutting his teeth on. *Sharon and Karen* was the first video they would work on together.

Gender was applying Kane's and Dior's makeup when there was a knock at the studio door. It was Tony Davis, who wanted to introduce his new friend Nick Iacona to LaRue; he knew LaRue was looking for new talent. They were duly introduced, and LaRue was instantly smitten, on both a personal and professional level. He fluttered back to where Kane and Dior were being made up: "My God, you've got to see this boy—he looks just like Tom Cruise!" He had handsome if unspectacular bones, a fine but not noticeably muscled body. But his skin had the glow of a movie star's, and his eyes were exceptionally beautiful, a distinctive light blue-green that contrasted dramatically with his full brown hair. It was all set off by a becoming shyness; he hardly spoke. LaRue couldn't stop. He was visibly nervous, and the gods of love were in a cruelly impish mood: When he flopped into a director's chair, it collapsed beneath him—an overweight person's nightmare under any circumstances and the very last stunt one wants to perform before a newfound object of affection. They went ahead with the box-cover shoot, snapping a straightforward shot for the front, with Dior looking remarkably female in his white bikini, one hip hitched up provocatively. For the back, Kane, with layered hair bleached to within an inch of its life, pointed a single white fingernail at the surprising contents of Dior's bikini bottom, staring into the camera, her mouth an O of mock horror.

LaRue ordered test shots of Iacona; Dior snagged a Polaroid to take home ("I kept one because he was so cute and sweet; it was so new to me, and I wanted pictures of all my new friends"). LaRue wasn't taking any chances. He had been in the business long enough to know a godsend when he saw it. Young men of Iacona's caliber were not to be found on street corners, although that was essentially where Iacona had come from. If a director were lucky, he might find a boy of Iacona's knockout looks after a long and carefully orchestrated search. Iacona had come looking for LaRue, and LaRue—smitten or not—knew a good thing when he saw it. He more or less guaranteed Iacona a career in the industry, immediately arranging to put him in *Sharon and Karen* and offering to personally squire him around town and introduce him to the players in the business. He also invited Iacona to stay with him, since Iacona was still living at the Saharan Motor Hotel and even a motel of a lesser order was more than he could afford.

It's not an exaggeration to say that the day Iacona met LaRue and Kane and Dior was a turning point in his young life. In fact, it was a turning point in all their lives. It was as if a spell had been cast in the studio that afternoon, and a web of emotional, sexual, and spiritual connections among the group began to take shape. These connections would sometimes feed into their unorthodox line of work, sometimes spring from the work itself, and occasionally create conflict that hampered it. LaRue's frank adoration of Iacona was the first string in the web, and it would remain one of the strongest. A sudden intimacy had also sprung up between the title performers of *Sharon and Karen* as well, a connection that both found a little unnerving. "Sharon and I had a date after we made the movie," recalls Dior. "I had dated a woman, then dated men, then met another woman; when I met Sharon I had been attracted only to men for a while, but I was really attracted to her, so I decided I was bisexual. Our attraction was really intense; it was a really strong, electric thing." Says Kane: "There was something between us; I was really terrified. I could feel that he really loved me, and I was afraid he would want something from me that I couldn't give him. I avoided him for a while, but eventually we became great friends."

And while both Kane and Dior had found Iacona handsome, they were at first more interested in Tony Davis. Dior and Davis dated for a while, but the relationship was fairly brief. The connection between Kane and Iacona, meanwhile, was forged during the filming of their scene in *Sharon and Karen*. In the video Dior plays "ace TV reporter Wally Wissit," who goes undercover—as a woman, though one isn't quite sure why—to expose an underground sex club "right in the heart of Minneapolis, Minnesota." In the opening scene, Dior, in a teased red wig and rather frightful faux-denim midriff-baring ensemble, spies Susan Vegas propositioning two men in a Jacuzzi. (The men, by process of elimination, must be Steve Vegas—a distant cousin, perhaps?—and one Mic Freeze.) "This is going to be the story of the year!" she whispers breathlessly into her tape recorder before being surprised by Kane and Davis. She flees their inquisitive looks ("Strange chick, let me tell ya," says Davis). The camera returns to the Jacuzzi for a while before moving on to the sparsely furnished gym, where Iacona and Andrew Michaels are doing push-ups in unison. Kane, in pink bikini, joins the workout, although they don't linger on abdominals for long and are soon going at it with remarkable enthusiasm on a sheet of black plastic. Meanwhile, Dior—or Wally—presumably overcome by the atmosphere, takes a break from sleuthing to toddle off to the bathroom, now in heels and pink-and-green bikini, to entertain himself for a while. LaRue's camera lingers on the paradoxes of anatomy and attire, crawling from a patent-leather pump-clad foot up a shapely, apparently hairless leg to arrive—surprise!—at an engorged penis peeking out of a woman's bikini as it is lovingly massaged by a ferocious set of pink Lee Pressons. The video cuts between the three scenes for a while, and what's most notable is the mechanical nature of the interaction between Ms. Vegas and her two partners, who are obviously straight and interested only in being serviced, and the outlandish energy of the trio of Kane, Iacona, and Michaels, who are apparently having a good—if confusing—time; all three are up for anything and more or less accomplish it. After a lesbian encounter between Kane and Susan Vegas, in which Kane gives a convincing impression of being a WTW—woman-to-woman—virgin, the video closes with Wally Wissit being exposed, figuratively and very literally. Kane and Davis come upon a sleeping Dior.

KANE: I know I know that girl!

DAVIS: I've been trying to meet her all weekend.

(Dior shifts in his sleep; the ace reporter's disguise does not extend, apparently, to undergarments, and all is exposed)

KANE: Fuck! It's a guy!

DAVIS: Fuck! I didn't want to meet her that bad!

(Kane snags the tape recorder)

KANE: Fuck! It's Wally Wissit, schlock TV reporter!

The sleeping beauty awakes, and another marathon three-way ensues. All seem energetic to the end, with the notable exception of Dior's wig, which gets rather wilted by the finale. LaRue in voice-over provides the finish: Wally's hard work was not in vain; his exposé of Sex Club '89 was indeed the story of the year.

Although she had performed in literally hundreds of X-rated movies and was not particularly susceptible to forming emotional attachments to costars, Sharon Kane fell for Nick Iacona during their admittedly unusual coupling on video. "I was smitten with him the day we worked together. I did a scene with him and Andrew Michaels. I had to have a strap-on and fuck him, and I don't think I'd ever done that before," she says musingly of the experience. One would imagine it to be difficult to forget. "He brought his own; I remember being amazed at how big it was. I thought he was an amazing performer—he was quite relaxed about it. That's when I fell in love with him." It may not have been a stroll in the moonlight or even dinner and a movie, but a deep connection had been forged between Kane and Iacona during their romp with Mr. Michaels on black plastic. Kane, like LaRue, responded to something in Iacona that moved deep beneath the surface of his smashing looks and aggressive sexuality, an almost child-like sensitivity that was only rarely exposed. "He had a lot of heart," Kane says. "And it was almost like you could put your hand in his chest and feel it there."

What's most astonishing about the layers of connections among the group is that the complexities of their romantic or emotional or sexual attachments didn't destroy their friendships; on the contrary, they became a tight-knit group that worked hard together—and played even harder. LaRue and Kane both felt enormous affection for Iacona, but there was no jealousy between them; they remained great friends. Perhaps because they had sex—or orchestrated it—for a living, they didn't overvalue its importance as a validation of an emotional or spiritual bond. LaRue's love for Iacona wasn't lessened because it was never physically consummated. And though Kane and Iacona slept together on occasion, it wasn't a prerequisite for their intimacy. As Kane puts it, the dynamic of the group was stronger than anything else. "It started this whole eye-of-a-cyclone thing," Kane says. "We instantly became an inseparable group. The energy between all of us was really strong."

For Iacona, the friendships forged during the making of *Sharon and Karen* would be an important source of emotional support over the years, although time and circumstances would put strains on his relationships with Davis and Kane and Dior and LaRue. But perhaps more important, the meeting with Chi Chi and Co. brought him closer to realizing his ambitions of making a success of himself. His youth had been an unhappy one; the only way he'd been able to escape it was through drugs, but the drugs quickly became the thing he needed to escape. He'd also found solace in sex and learned early that it could also be a source of income.

Just as the amateur actor dreams of movie stardom and the small-town reporter imagines nailing the next Watergate, Nick the street hustler had looked to a career in gay porn as the ultimate achievement in the field—sex for sale—he found himself in. Meeting LaRue would be the key that opened the door. He was the man who would make Iacona's dreams come true. As he stood on the threshold of a new career, Iacona probably imagined, as young people in all walks of life do, that realizing his dreams would make him happy, would fill the hole in the world that his father's death had created, that years of hard living had deepened. Gay men and women perhaps arrive at adulthood with a larger store of hopes than their straight counterparts; many have been denied the primary pleasures of adolescence and look to adulthood for the fulfillment of several years' worth of deferred dreams. They may also be more vulnerable to the disappointments that await them.

CHAPTER FOUR

B ut before his dreams of porn stardom could come true, before he could begin making major money in his new career, indeed even before *Sharon and Karen* could be rushed into release, Nick Iacona had to cease being Nick Iacona. A new name—and with it a new persona—had to be devised. One hates to rend the veil of illusions from a believer's eyes, but Ryan Idol, to pick a notable example, is not the man's real name. There is, of course, a basic reason for performers taking noms de porn: It gives them a veneer of anonymity, and porn has always been a line of work that lies outside the bounds of social respectability. Using a fake name also works as a kind of psychological tool that enables performers to pursue a career that they may be ambivalent about; on some level it was not Nick Iacona at all who became a porn star, but a young man born twenty years after Iacona's birth named Joey Stefano.

LaRue had by late 1989 begun to establish a name as a gay video director and had regained the attention of his ex-employers at Catalina. He took his new discovery by the offices one afternoon, and there a name was chosen. Catalina's Chris Mann suggested the faux surname; he thought Iacona resembled a Catalina stable stud name Tony Stefano. It's not unusual for the last names of successful porn stars to be stolen for performers who may or may not resemble them. Thus Ryan Idol begat Tony Idol. A veritable pack of Foxes have worked in gay porn at one time or another: putative brothers Scott and Guy, and Michael, Sean, Allan, Jeremy, Steve, Christian, Dylan… The list stretches back for a couple of decades, presumably to when the word was a generic term for a handsome man. LaRue gave Iacona his new given name, Joey, and the decision was made.

But if Catalina was happy to take a look at LaRue's new discovery, both LaRue and Stefano would have to prove themselves before the porn powerhouses would give them their stamp of approval. Fortunately, the frenetic pace at which porn videos are produced made it easy to get one's work seen, and LaRue, acting as a gay porn Von Sternberg, with Stefano his Dietrich, got quickly to work. Immediately after the meeting on the *Sharon and Karen* set, LaRue cast Stefano in the video *Buddy System II: Camouflage* for Vivid Video.

Wanting to expose Iacona to the mechanics of shooting a porn video, LaRue brought him on a visit to the set of an In-Hand shoot. Working as an actor on the film was Gino Colbert, an aspiring director who had already met Iacona through Tony Davis. In fact, Colbert had hoped to use Iacona in a movie he had been setting up when LaRue called to ask that he not use him. LaRue went on to explain that he was planning to mastermind a major campaign around Stefano and didn't want Colbert to spoil his plans; Colbert agreed.

Watching Stefano wander the set that afternoon, Colbert began to think that directing him, in fact, might not be quite as enjoyable as, say, performing with him. In a pair of sweatpants that accentuated the positive, he was fairly irresistible. Though Colbert had a scene to shoot in a matter of minutes, he reasoned that a warm-up would not be out of order, and soon he and Stefano were in each other's arms—giving an impromptu audition, as it turned out, for LaRue, who happened upon them. "That's hot! That's hot!" Colbert remembers LaRue saying. "If you can do that, I'll use you both in a scene next week!"

But such are the pitfalls of the business that when Colbert and Stefano were reunited a week later on the set of *Buddy System II,* Colbert found it difficult to perform. "It was a disaster," he says. "I didn't have sex for three or four days before, thinking that my body would function better. It didn't work. I had trouble getting hard. We did everything in the scene—oral, kissing—but when it came time to fuck, I could not get hard." And that is, of course, the most common—and sometimes insurmountable, as it were—problem plaguing porn sets. "I was making up all these excuses in my mind," Colbert continues. "Was it because I was too anxious? Because I didn't have sex before?" It's a question that has rattled around in the minds of almost all porn actors on some occasion.

In the end Colbert used a rather unimpressive rubber stand-in for the scene in question. Set in an imaginary barracks whose unusual accoutrement include hardwood floors and a leather sling, the movie is no miracle of verisimilitude—the boys sport rather exotic tan lines for Army recruits. The film is generally unspectacular. Stefano shares top billing with Ryan Yeager, though on the box, whose graphics are infinitely more sophisticated than those in the film, it's INTRODUCING JOEY STEPHAN. He appears with Yeager in the minimal con-

necting scenes, as a G.I. swapping stories of sexual esca-
pades; neither has the makings of a Brando, but their three-
way scene, with Andrew Michaels, is a fairly sensational
finale. Its amusing rawness is enhanced by the unwieldy
decor—the sling is positioned above a pile of tires that the
actors have to clamber over awkwardly—and LaRue's voice
can be heard urging the actors on: "That's really good!" "OK,
start goin' for it..."

A slew of LaRue productions starring Stefano followed in
the closing months of 1989 and early 1990; LaRue recalls
filming a movie a week with his new star. Because he had
been a porn aficionado, Stefano had a laundry list of favorite
porn hunks he wanted to work with, and it was in LaRue's
interest to cater to his desires: the stronger the attraction, the
better the sex. "He would rattle off lists of names of guys he'd
want to have sex with," LaRue remembers, "but they were
mostly guys from way back, like Jack Wrangler, Cole Car-
penter, Eric Manchester, and Chad Douglas." Many weren't
working in the business anymore, but LaRue did what he
could. Stefano's type, generally speaking, was big, beefy, and
bruising. As he told *Thrust* magazine, "Butch, big, hairy, mus-
cular, older. That's my type." He used virtually the same
words in talking to *Manshots*: "Real butch, rough, manly,
dominant men. And I like older guys."

Jon Vincent was an actor Stefano had lusted after who fit
that bill, and LaRue cast them together in *Hard Knocks*. Other
In-Hand titles cranked out in quick succession included *Flexx
II: Pumping Up, To the Bone, French Kiss,* and *Fond Focus.*
(The latter film's title, which is an unusually delicate one for
a gay porn flick and has little bearing on the movie itself, is a
telling comment on the relationship between LaRue and Stefano.) The videos were by and large, in LaRue's words, "no-
budget" productions, but he managed to charm some of the

industry's most viable talent into doing for $500 for him what they would make three times that doing for others.

As Stefano's manager, chaperone, and confidant, LaRue had more or less exclusive control over Stefano's professional services, and he kept Stefano to himself for as long as he could. It was a matter both of professional savvy and personal obsession; separating the two instincts was impossible. But LaRue had made many important contacts while working in marketing and promotion at Catalina, and these friends and associates began inquiring about Stefano's availability for their productions. One who came calling was producer Jeff Appel at Vivid Video, a major straight-porn production company that had started up a gay line. Although almost all gay porn product is shot in a studio or a house made available for the purpose, occasionally video makers are subject to Cecil B. DeMille–like aspirations and try to vary the anonymity of their productions with exotic locales.

Appel and director Jim Steel were in such a mood when LaRue agreed to lend them the use of Stefano for their new video, an opus called *The River* that turned out to be an experience more redolent of Irwin Allen than Mr. DeMille. It was the first—and last—time Steel, who had been working in the business for several years, ventured out of the comfort of his studio. But hopes were high as cast and crew headed to Lake Havasu near the California-Arizona border for ten days of filming on a fifty-foot boat. The filming crew consisted of Steel, producer Appel, Patrick Dennis, and cameraman Richard Morgan. Also along for the ride was LaRue—"as the cook"—and, in the George Kennedy role, the captain Steel had hired to man the boat, who brought along an assistant.

The first unpleasant discovery to be made was that a fifty-foot boat, whose dimensions had seemed boundless in Steel's imagination, was in fact, as Steel glumly recalls, "not big." With two ten-foot decks on either side of a thirty-foot main cabin consisting of a small dining area, a bathroom, and two small cabins holding four beds each, things were going to be rather cramped aboard the S.S. *Homosex*. Also a bold experiment was the idea of assembling a video's entire cast for such an extended period; the normal procedure would have been to bring in the required duos or trios one at a time, film their scene, and send them home. Through the rosy haze of retrospect, Steel recalls that it was actually genial to have the boys "get to know each other" during the course of the shoot, rather than just perform the required sex acts on cue. But circumstances worked fairly quickly to undo any air of camaraderie that happened to develop.

Bad idea number one was Appel's admonition barring all the boys from participating in any extracurricular sexual activity. The only person to whom this did not apply, Steel recalls dryly, was Appel himself. Nor was there to be any drinking or drug-taking on the high seas, a sensible—and legally necessary—edict that nevertheless was not conducive to high spirits for a group of boys largely used to regular imbibing. With sex and drinking off-limits as diversions, how did the performers entertain themselves when they weren't filming scenes? "They didn't," Steel says. Filling the void were ego and attitude.

"They couldn't get along," says Steel. "You've got a couple of guys saying, 'I'm really straight, and I'm just doing this for the money.' That went over really big with the rest of them. Chi Chi being the cook was a drama in itself. It was like being on the S.S. *Minnow*—but with just a whole bunch of Gingers. By day three, everybody already hated each other, and then we had to go, 'OK, now you have to fuck!' Tempers were strained."

They managed to keep the video cameras rolling, even as the already strained atmosphere became increasingly tense under the daily 115-degree heat.

"We were in a goddamned floating tin can," as Steel puts it. "There was no air-conditioning. With that many guys doing a movie, the toilet backed up about day three." While shooting a scene with Stefano and Steve Kennedy going at it in a dinghy, the cameraman lost his footing, and the lone video camera—worth some $50,000—cracked in half. "And we're in bumfuck nowhere," Steel continues. "We had to go to the town, called the Town at the End of the Road, and call our camera company to have something airlifted in the next day. There was another $450."

Just as things got back on track, the captain's assistant had the first in a series of epileptic seizures, an unnerving if not dangerous distraction; the captain hadn't mentioned his assistant's condition. Shortly after this, news came over the public address system that the captain's trailer had mysteriously burned to the ground. He had rented it to friends—and "there was a baby involved," Steel recalls with dismay.

Through it all, Stefano had remained among the better sports. He and LaRue bickered repeatedly, but it was scarcely noticeable among the general air of contretemps. He alone among the cast and crew seemed to find eternal amusement in the chaos that seemed to be a constant of the shoot. Steel, who had maintained a certain amount of equilibrium throughout the proceedings, was finally brought to the breaking point on the last day of the shoot. (He'd maintained his even keel by occasionally commandeering the Jet Ski to zip into the Town at the End of the Road and spend a few hours on the stool at the end of the bar at the village's one and only drinking establishment.) One actor, who had caused endless delays due to his inability to climax despite a week of encouragement, was ultimately the cause of Steel's temperamental undoing. The actor and Stefano had been doing a dialogue scene in a tent, which Steel was shooting from some distance away. When they were asked to do a third take, the actor petulantly turned to Stefano and said, "If he were a better director, we wouldn't have to do so many takes." He failed to recall—"he was dumb as a post," says Steel—that the tent was wired into Steel's headphones. "I'm told I hit the ground only once as I jumped the air and landed with my hands around his throat," Steel says. "I had been keeping everyone in line all week by behaving coolly, but I completely lost it. And everybody was really shocked—except Joey, who couldn't stop laughing. He thought it was the funniest thing he'd ever seen. I knew we'd be friends from that."

And so the filming of *The River* drew to a close, and the video joined the quickly growing ranks of Stefano's early oeuvre—in his first three months working he made twelve videos.

With a volume of product to promote, LaRue began campaigning. He brought to the charge not only his considerable experience in the marketing end of the business but also, and most important, his persona. He had been polishing his drag act—Gender was one of the first drag queens to advocate live singing rather than lip-synching and had encouraged him to follow his lead—and his performing skills stood him in good stead when it came to putting over his new discovery. Dave Kinnick, *Advocate Men*'s adult-film reviewer and reporter from 1988 to 1994, recalls LaRue's promotional savvy as a breath of fresh air in an industry whose major players took a more passive approach to the selling of their product. "Chi Chi was one of the people who, when she first started, was interested in pleasing the critics; she would court people like me in terms of traditional Hollywood promotion."

LaRue called the editors of the skin magazines and pitched Stefano, even traveling to New York, marching into editors' offices with layouts in hand, to win Stefano the covers of the key magazines: *Inches, Mandate, All Man.* (*Advocate Men*'s April 1990 issue featured a pouting Joey and the ludicrous cover line JAZZ PIANIST JOEY STEFANO PLAYS WITH BOTH HANDS; Stefano had probably never been in the same room with a piano. And jazz, no less!) LaRue lobbied successfully to get Stefano on the cover of the first *Adam Gay Video Directory,* a comprehensive annual review of the year's gay porn releases.

They also continued the campaign after hours, using the gay social scene to display Stefano's appeal. Unlike many actors in either adult or Hollywood films, Stefano looked just as sensational when the spotlight was turned off. "It was kind of like the movie *The Girl Can't Help It,* when Jayne Mansfield's agent took her out to club after club after club," recalls Kinnick. "That was how Chi Chi marketed Joey; he was the first person she made it a point to drag around to all these clubs and introduce him—not so much as a big new star but as a friend who happened to be also doing movies; a lot of people also got the vague impression that he was her boyfriend.

"It was clear that there was real affection between them. I've seen other directors drag boys around town on leashes, and it looks like they're being kept in line with the right drugs. That was not the case with Joey. He wasn't a bright kid; she'd park him at a table and buy him cocktails, while Chi Chi would find people to talk to. Chi Chi was always very good at promoting her work through her social life and vice versa."

But no amount of promotion can sell a bad product, and from the beginning it was clear that Joey Stefano would have been a phenomenon in the industry even without the charm and connections of Chi Chi LaRue behind him. Even his earliest, cheapest videos reveal a man whose combination of traditionally masculine good looks and languidly magnetic sexuality rivet the attention. His almost-hairless olive-skinned body wasn't gym-sculpted; it had a tinge of feminine softness to it, amusingly at odds with the screaming-skull tattoo on his right shoulder that he had acquired before tattoos became de rigueur for gay men of his generation. His full head of dark hair and classically shaped eyebrows set off the green in his eyes. The nose was just a little too full, but it gave his face a defining toughness; the thick Philly accent didn't jar when that nose was taken into account. If his penis was ample and attractive, by no means deficient in size but not stellar, his ass was his fortune. Pert and perfectly rounded, it swaggered naturally when he walked, as if advertising its expertise, and on video it remained shapely in all manner of positions. It was all animated by an erotic energy that was almost aggressive in its voraciousness, though Stefano preferred to play the technically passive sexual roles. That combination was his trademark, and it was one that rocketed him in record time to the top of the industry.

Whether it was before the cameras or after hours, Stefano was working diligently. But the pressures of his burgeoning porn career—or the temptations it brought his way—began to chip away at his resolve to remain drug-free. Just a few weeks after he hit town, he met Doug Smith at Numbers, a middlebrow hustler bar whose longevity has made it something of a West Hollywood institution. Smith had a spectacularly checkered past to match Stefano's. He'd grown up in Hollywood, Florida, where his parents had institutionalized him at age ten after being unable to stop the boy from sneaking out of the house to seduce security guards on construction sites. He spent much of his adolescence in rebellion against various correctional institutions, before joining the Navy at seventeen. He was more interested in the sailors than the sea, and when he'd run through all the likely candidates on ship he went AWOL from his Virginia base to try his luck in New York. He hustled tricks at the piers for a month before deciding that even a barrack was more palatable than living indefinitely on the streets and returned to his base, where he was soon given an honorable discharge. Back in New York he worked the hustler bars for a couple of years, lived with a friend who was dying of AIDS complications, and eventually departed for parts west, spending some time in Australia before landing in L.A. He was hustling at Numbers when he met Stefano, who was there with a former porn star named Michael Gere. Though Smith found Stefano withdrawn and a little uppity (he remembers thinking, *Who's this queen with the big butt who thinks she's going to be a big porn star?*), a few days later he picked up Stefano at the Saharan motel for a trip to the beach. Once there, he took out a joint and offered it to Stefano, who declined, explaining that he'd only recently gotten out of rehab and had been clean for a year and a half. Smith got ready for an Al-Anon spiel, but none was forthcoming. Stefano seemed at ease with his decision and didn't seem bothered by Smith's smoking.

They lost touch for a couple of months, as Stefano moved from the motel to an apartment in Gino Colbert's building on Whitley Avenue in Hollywood, thence a month later to LaRue's for a short stay, finally settling with Tony Davis at the Confetti Apartments on Martel Avenue. The modern gray complex with "fun" bright red metal trim was the sort of new apartment block that clogged West Hollywood streets, replacing individual homes and duplexes with sprawling buildings with greater financial capacities. But the Confetti Apartments weren't quite in West Hollywood—they were a little to the less desirable east and a little too close to an unsavory stretch of Sunset Boulevard. They did have fireplaces, microwaves, balconies, a spa, a fitness center, and a sauna, as a billboard in front states, and the building became home to a number of adult-film names and would for a while be known by the gay-porn cognoscenti as the Porn Palace.

Smith caught up with Stefano the day he and Davis moved in and was somewhat awed by the sight of a quartet of male porn stars—Michael Gere and a performer named Michael Moore were also in attendance—wandering around in various states of undress, arranging the new black faux-leather furniture Stefano had just purchased. It spelled success to the eyes of a small-town Florida boy and was probably gratifying to the boy from Chester, Pennsylvania, too. They had both spent time on the streets and knew the peculiar thrill that acquiring possessions could supply. A couch and a rented apartment in a borderline neighborhood isn't exactly a house with a mortgage, but to a young man who had scraped by living on the streets of New York, it was tangible proof of success.

The pleasure of his new success may have awakened memories of other highs; Stefano was having a good time, and it may have seemed perverse to limit his pleasures, so he began drinking again. Smith was startled one day when Stefano asked him to pick up a bottle of peach schnapps on his way over. They made drinks, and Smith felt a rush of guilt; he did not ask Stefano why he had started drinking again, but he felt uneasy—and protective. Smith had started dealing a form of speed known colloquially as crystal, and he tried strenuously at first to keep Stefano from mixing with the friends and clients he was dealing to. He would run into Stefano at clubs and act rudely, hoping to keep him away from his associates.

LaRue too was startled by Stefano's sudden decision to start drinking again. They had taken a trip to New York together.

LaRue was doing a drag show at a club, and Stefano came along for the ride. Stefano took the train to Philadelphia one day to visit his family, returning in a dark mood. As soon as he got back to the apartment where he and LaRue were crashing, he went out again, returning a few minutes later with a bottle of vodka and a bottle of peach schnapps. With one in each hand, he started drinking. LaRue was dismayed. "I said, 'What are you doing?'" LaRue recalls. "'I'm fine. I'm fine,' he said. I think I tried to pry them out of his hands." They sat in awkward silence for a while; LaRue didn't know what else to do. But it was not the beginning of a drastic binge. Stefano drank for a while, enough to blunt whatever pain his visit to Philadelphia had awakened, and then they went out for dinner, and then they came home and went to bed.

Back in L.A., conflict began to simmer between Davis and Stefano. Davis had sponsored Stefano's move to L.A.; he had been his initial entrée into the porn world, and now he was beginning to be upstaged by his own protégé. Davis had been in the business for several years and made scores of videos, but he had never reached the upper echelons of the industry that Stefano was quickly on the verge of attaining. Living in the same apartment certainly didn't mitigate the tension. Davis had been used to Stefano's relying on him for advice and opinions, and he continued to dispense them, although Stefano began to resist. The attention he was garnering naturally boosted his self-confidence, and he started rebelling against Davis's dictating to him. A pair of porn starlets in the same apartment was probably a bad idea in the first place; with both egos in full flower, there was hardly room for the microwave. Davis, who was also put off by Stefano's increasing drug use, decided to move out.

The vacancy was quickly filled by Smith, who was happy to move into what he perceived as a "glam apartment with a porn star." He had begun making considerable sums dealing crystal and was passing his days and nights as a courtier to a group of young men who called themselves the "West Hollywood showgirls." In retrospect, Smith has a more precise description: "Basically, they were crystal addicts." But they were beautiful crystal addicts, and they granted honorary showgirl membership to boys who could supply needed services—hairdressers, designers, and, of course, drug dealers. Some had sugar daddies; many had no visible means of support; all had extensive wardrobes. Smith was granted group membership because of his crystal connection.

For a while Smith and Stefano, two boys with hardscrabble backgrounds, were living the homo life of Riley. They had both experienced "West Hollywood culture shock," having grown up with no thought of ever attending art school and reaching adulthood with a shockingly underdeveloped fashion sense. Fortunately, it's not hard to get the hang of a tank top; and LaRue was an endless supply of style tips, telling Stefano what to buy and where to buy it.

LaRue's and Stefano's was a strange relationship that all who knew them would later classify as "dysfunctional," though at the time the term wasn't in common parlance. LaRue was working tirelessly to further Stefano's career—putting him in video after video, working the phones to garner magazine publicity, introducing him to the powers that be. And his attentions were partially fueled by his emotional attachment to Stefano. Gender, who did "makeup and motivation" on all LaRue's early movies and observed their interpersonal dynamics, says, "Nick never would have gotten the buildup that he did if it weren't for Larry's personal interest. Larry needed Nick's adoration and knew what he could give in trade." If he could not have Stefano's unconditional love and uncourted attention, he'd take a less pure form of attachment. All the work he was arranging for Stefano naturally created a bond of obligation on Stefano's part; he knew how much LaRue was doing for him and knew that part of LaRue's motivation was a kind of love that he couldn't reciprocate. Says LaRue: "I was in love, and I was obsessed; he knew it and used it to his advantage. I told him every day, 'I love you, and you're killing me.' But I was obviously not his type; I was a fat drag queen—I wasn't a hairy muscleman."

Karen Dior watched the development of their relationship with bewilderment: "Larry was quickly saying, 'I'm in love with Nick, and it's not good.'" But LaRue couldn't keep away from Stefano—and didn't want to. "They were very close," Dior continues. "And Nick loved Larry, but not in the same way. Nick would also manipulate Larry, because Larry loved him and he could get him to do things that Larry wouldn't do for anyone else. Larry won't lift a finger for anyone, because he doesn't have to—he is always surrounded by his porn slaves. He won't go to the grocery store without an entourage. But he would drive Nick to the airport all the time; when they went to a movie, Nick picked the movie."

But the benefits of the relationship were by no means all Stefano's. In putting his talents to use to make Stefano into a porn star, LaRue was not acting out of blind love, foisting an unbankable commodity on the public in order to win the reward of Stefano's everlasting gratitude. He knew that Stefano was a beautiful young man who was also an amazingly adept sexual performer. "He was born for this business," LaRue says. The attention accorded to Stefano's beauty and talent was just as beneficial to LaRue's career as it was to Stefano's. Stefano was LaRue's personal discovery, and everyone in the business knew it. LaRue was acting as his unofficial manager, and all who wanted to work with him—and soon everyone did—had to go through LaRue to obtain his services. The bigger Stefano became, the more power LaRue wielded.

But their relationship was by no means just a matter of mutual usefulness; theirs was a real bond that would last in some form until Stefano's death. LaRue, the fat boy from Minnesota who had blossomed into the fat drag queen from West Hollywood, had captured the attention of a man of almost perfect beauty. For a while he had Stefano's emotional and professional fidelity and was resigned to living without the sexual attention. Stefano had found in Paciotti a father figure and in LaRue a mother figure, if you will. "Nick wanted Larry to be his buddy and his mama," Dior says. Like a parent, LaRue gave Stefano his undivided love, something the boy whose father had died at a crucial age deeply needed. "They needed each other so desperately," says Gender. "The most gorgeous people are often the most insecure, and Nick was very insecure."

Sharon Kane sums up the delicate balance of their friendship simply: "For both of them, it was a blessing and a curse." Indeed, that Stefano saw LaRue as a parental figure meant that his store of anger at a father who had deserted him was taken out on LaRue. "He lived for the attention I gave him," says LaRue, "but he used it against me. He put me through hell—and to this day I don't really know why. It was hard for him to express things. He held a lot of things in."

In a short time—a matter of the summer turning to fall—Stefano had gone from scrambling a living on the streets of New York to being an up-and-comer in gay porn, ensconced in a new apartment, pulling in $500 to $1,000 for a day's work. But his new life hadn't kept him from falling into old habits, and Stefano managed to navigate the considerable distance from peach schnapps to PCP in a trice. Angel dust, as PCP is commonly called, had been Stefano's favorite drug in Philadelphia, and on a trip to visit his family that fall of '89, he scored some and got on the phone with Smith. Out came a flood of confused emotion. Smith could hear Stefano sobbing as he tried to explain why he had decided not to come back to L.A. "He thought he had disappointed people like Tony and Larry," Smith recalls. "He was scared that people didn't like him, that he had acted like a jerk. The thing with Tony got to him; I know he felt really guilty about what had happened." He felt he had lost a friend in Davis, that he had failed him; he was afraid of failing LaRue too, because he couldn't continue to let him run his life. He knew that he was causing LaRue unhappiness but couldn't stop himself. He wailed that "everyone was trying to run his life," Smith says. "He was disappointed that everything wasn't perfect." He said he wanted to kill himself.

Smith tried to calm him down, telling him to come back. "I said, 'You're doing fabulous. Everyone wants to be you.'" In the end Stefano didn't need much convincing to come back. The suicide threat seemed to be a fairly perfunctory cry for attention. After all, what promise did life in Philadelphia hold out for him? On his first trip back from California, he had returned to drastic drug use. And he had no source of funds to support it. In L.A., at least, he was making good money. If life there wasn't what he had imagined it to be, it was still a distinct improvement on his previous existence.

But back in L.A. he couldn't shake the blues as the holidays approached. It was a sad season for him, the time of his birthday and his father's death. "That first Christmas he was in a deep depression," Smith remembers. "We had made a lot of friends in the building, and we all got together to make dinner. But Nick didn't want to eat. He wouldn't talk to anybody, and he wouldn't talk about why; he sulked. The neighbors were pissed because they had made a nice cake." Later Stefano told Smith that he had been thinking about his father's death, that he was used to being with his family at Christmas. Even the cocker spaniel Stefano had bought on an impulse seemed to be conspiring to blacken his mood. She insisted on defecating freely all over the Porn Palace's pristine carpeting. Life wasn't perfect indeed.

CHAPTER FIVE

The biggest star in the gay-porn pantheon—in the figurative sense, if not the anatomic—is Jeff Stryker. It is likely that he will remain the most famous gay-porn performer because the exigencies of the business have changed drastically in the years since he established his stardom, and most industry watchers agree that it would be impossible today to create a star on the Stryker scale. Stryker was pulled from obscurity in central Illinois by producer-director John Travis, who had been sent photos of the man-who-would-be-Stryker by an amateur photographer. He saw potential in the baby-faced brunet and sponsored his trip to Los Angeles. Travis and fellow director Matt Sterling chose a name for their new protégé and gave him a makeover to enhance his appeal to the target community: Out went the distressingly unfashionable parted-in-the-middle hair, the less-than-perfect teeth, the unimpressive pectorals. In came a full-body tan covering a pumped-to-perfection body, a calculated, smoldering image mixing "a little bit of a young Elvis Presley and a young Marlon Brando," as Sterling put it in a 1989 interview in *The Advocate* magazine. And with the 1986 release of his first movie, Sterling's *Bigger Than Life,* a star was instantly born. Stryker's name would become almost synonymous with gay porn over the next few years, although he made relatively few films during the period, working exclusively for Travis and Sterling, with whom he had successive personal relationships. He went on to produce his own features and also branched out into the bisexual and straight video markets. His endowment became so well-known that he was approached by a company to have it immortalized in rubber, though he later expressed dismay at the liberties taken. "From what they say, it's the best-selling dildo in the history of dildos," he said in the same issue of *The Advocate* in which Sterling was quoted (one seriously doubts, however, that accurate sales figures have ever been compiled). "They added nothing in width from the mold of my dick, but they added an inch in length. It insults me that they did that."

The successful manufacturing and marketing of Jeff Stryker became the yardstick against which all others in the gay porn business would be measured. That Joey Stefano reached the top echelon of the industry in 1990 can be gauged by the fact that he worked for all three architects of the Stryker phenomenon that year—Travis, Sterling, and Stryker himself. Indeed, LaRue's tireless campaigning and Stefano's unflagging sexual enthusiasm had begun to pay off. Catalina, the company that LaRue had been forced to leave in order to forge a directing career, was now very much interested in his new protégé and hired LaRue to direct his new star in a movie titled *Billboard.* The perfunctory plot unfolds in a painting studio, where Stefano, playing the boss, is working on a billboard for "Jock" underwear. The video is more polished than those of LaRue's earlier oeuvre: The camerawork is smooth, the director's voice isn't heard exhorting his actors to try a new position, and the cast are all impeccably tanned and coiffed to the nines. Stefano performs ably in three scenes, although his first two partners, Adam Grant and Vic Summers, are rather bland. He seems particularly inspired in his last scene, a three-way with Lon Flexx and Chris Stone (who despite his Anglo moniker breaks into authentic-sounding Spanish at moments of inspiration). The movie's chief significance is simply the imprimatur it gave both Stefano and LaRue; they'd moved from the second-rank production companies to the first. But true to form, Catalina insisted that LaRue use yet another pseudonym for the movie. If Chi Chi LaRue the director was now considered Catalina material, Chi Chi LaRue the name was not. "It wasn't masculine," LaRue recalls. So a man named Taylor Hudson—culled from the surnames of Elizabeth and Rock (there's a masculine concept)—was credited with *Billboard* and indeed all of LaRue's Catalina releases for several years.

John Travis asked to work with Stefano on a Catalina video, and LaRue knew that working with Travis at Catalina would be key to cementing his status as a top-flight performer, so he encouraged Stefano to do the movie. *Hard Steal* stars Rod Phillips (whom Stefano was dating at the time) as a former jewel thief brought in to help corral a ring of intrepid practitioners of his past profession. The blond and boyish Phillips' bad acting is, perversely enough, truly stellar: His inability to recite the most rudimentary dialogue with conviction is mesmerizing. Stefano, on the other hand, is unusually convincing in his role as a call boy (which, to be sure, is not much of a stretch). Both the plotting and the direction of the video are more complex than is the norm. Travis makes the startling innovation of actually cutting away from a sex scene to advance the plot. While Stefano and Phillips get it on, a black-clad figure accessorized with ski mask and flashlight breaks into the condo; as Stefano groans on the sound track, the thief tiptoes past the Nagel poster, across the faux-tile flooring, and into a closet, whence he removes a briefcase containing the presumably priceless jewels. They clink cheaply as he fondles them outside, Catalina Video not having a jewel-loan agreement with Harry Winston.

But it was back to minimal plotting for Stefano's video for Matt Sterling. Sterling was preparing the debut of a new star, whom he had dubbed Ryan Idol, and he picked Stefano to costar in Idol's only sex scene (besides a solo number) in *Idol Eyes*. Written—barely—as a journey of self-discovery on the part of Mr. Idol, the video's scenes take place in a series of strange faux environments that match the starched perfection of the performers. The video's stylization and electronic music contrast oddly with the more traditional elements (i.e., the dialogue: "Suck that cock, man"). Idol wanders an unnamed island beach in a red Speedo, coming upon all manner of scandalous behavior that awakens in him some urges he can't resist. Viewers seduced by Idol's loutish beauty on the box cover probably wish he'd succumbed a little sooner, but the tease, as Sterling knows, is part of the appeal; the anticipation heightens the Idol aura, so when he finally does have sex with a man, the viewer is almost grateful. And his scene with Stefano is a standout, for aesthetic reasons alone. The video's production values and the beauty of the two principals combine to make for dazzling viewing. Their hair alone is breathtaking—and Idol's is generally more erect than his penis.

Joey Stefano had indisputably arrived. And his arrival as a gay porn superstar was a phenomenon the industry hadn't seen before for a single, significant reason: He was a "bottom"—the passive performer in anal sex, the active one in oral. The top rung of the industry had traditionally been occupied exclusively by "tops," men whose machismo would theoretically have been compromised by more versatile screen behavior. They dominated their partners; they were serviced. And it was believed that that was the way the gay porn audience liked its stars—remote, superior, and unequivocally "masculine." Indeed, half of the mystique of stars such as Jeff Stryker, Rex Chandler, and Ryan Idol is not just that they're masculine but that they are straight. Whether in fact they are or not is irrelevant; the image they project is what they are selling, and they and their handlers chose to sell an image of quasiheterosexuality. John R. Burger, in his 1994 book *One-Handed Histories: The Eroto-Politics of Gay Male Video Pornography,* writes of this phenomenon's growth in the years 1982 to 1988: "A hierarchization of porn stars begins to occur within the star system. This hierarchy, vanguarded by Travis and Sterling, positions straight-identified actors such as Rick Donovan, Brian Maxon, Tony Stefano, Tim Lowe, Matt Ramsey and Tom Brock—men who, infrequently, could get fucked for bucks, but would not be caught dead swallowing semen or kissing a buddy on the lips—at the top, and usually in the top's position, while the more obviously 'gay' performers (i.e., bottoms who enjoy being penetrated) are given a lesser status."

Dave Kinnick confirms the caste system that dominated the industry: "It was believed that the only people capable of being stars were these guys who were promoted as being straight; the mainstay of gay porn since day one had been these supposedly straight men fucking gay guys. The bottoms are never famous; the bottoms are interchangeable." He believes the popularity of such stars may be more attributable to the tastes of the video makers themselves than the consumers' preferences. "We don't know that the consumer buys into this completely," Kinnick continues. "The industry does not do market research. Trends in gay porn tend to be run by the subconscious of half a dozen key porn figures rather than any real research. Yes, Ryan Idol and Jeff Stryker movies sell the most, but is it because they are the consumers' favorites or because they have the biggest budgets and the best promotions? Which came first, the chicken or the egg?"

There is considerable evidence, anecdotal though it is, that many gay men find straight men more attractive than men who are perceptibly gay. Witness, for example, the ubiquity of the term "straight-acting" as a quality sought in respondents to personal ads. One can assess the appeal of straight men in gay erotica by looking at the thematic breakdown of films in the *Adam Gay Video 1991 Directory.* Professions receiving multiple depictions in gay video include athletes (71), construction workers (27), cops (19), cowboys (15), farmers (6), mechanics (9), military men (17), movers and haulers (5), repairmen (9), and men in uniform (25). Generally speaking, these are trades not noted for their gay-friendliness. Need it be added that there are no listings for films depicting occupations traditionally associated with gay men—the tally would be interior decorators (0), fashion designers (0), and hairdressers (0).

The reasons for some gay men's erotic fascination with straight men are probably a complex mixture of psychological and cultural factors. But the rise of the cult of heterosexual men in gay porn in the '80s may be linked to circumstances specific to the times: the spread of AIDS. Surely it is not coincidental that over the years in which fear of the disease—and the widespread homophobia it engendered—began to take root in the culture, gay men began to fetishize straight men in their video pornography to an unprecedented degree. A causal connection can probably never be proved, but it seems likely that on a subconscious level, fear of AIDS informed the fantasy of the straight man as the ideal love object.

But by the late '80s, gay men had suffered almost a decade of virulent attacks caused by the attention focused on the community by the AIDS epidemic. They had also watched with increasing frustration as the government dragged its feet over research and development of treatment for the disease. An explosion of activism was unleashed with the creation of the advocacy group AIDS Coalition to Unleash Power, or ACT UP, in 1987. It and the movements it spawned—the Queer Nation group and *OutWeek* magazine and its bull-terrier mouthpiece, Michelangelo Signorile—brought a new sense of urgency to gay men's lives. The media attention garnered by the controversy over the "outing" of public figures served most importantly to bring home to gay men the significance of the decision to keep their sexuality a secret. If the invisibility of gay figures in public life was no longer to be taken for granted, one's decision to stay in the closet suddenly seemed less defensible than it had before.

The popularity of Joey Stefano can partially be seen as a by-product of this new wave of activism sweeping gay culture. Whether it was on a conscious or subconscious level, consumers of gay porn were expanding their sexual horizons, granting icon status for the first time to a star who was almost exclusively a bottom. The hegemony of the top was toppled; a new mood had arrived.

Sabin, the editor of the *Gay Video Guide* and cocreator of the annual Gay Erotic Video Awards, saw Stefano's success as a significantly market-created phenomenon. "There was a new generation driving the market. These were kids coming out of the closet, joining ACT UP, who didn't want to worship some straight man. The fact that Joey was out and that he was obviously enjoying what he was doing made him the first bottom to break into superstar status. He was in the top four."

Dave Kinnick recalls the impact Stefano's new status as an openly gay, very public porn star had on the business: "The thing that was unique about Stefano was that here was this gay porn star actively courting the affections of men in public, something unheard of. It was shocking; he'd walk around at a club with a boy on his arm. The gay porn world has always been very insular, very backward. Then here comes Stefano, an aggressive bottom, who, to the extent he was capable of it, seemed very proud of being a bottom."

Indeed, one aspect of the new politicization of the gay community was a defiantly in-your-face attitude about gay sex. Gay activists weren't just writing legislation and marching on picket lines; they were storming straight bars and staging gay kiss-ins. Gay pornography thus took on a measure of political significance; the public renting or purchase of a gay porn video, after all, is an affirmation—to a small audience, certainly—of one's gay identity, one's membership in a community. Gay porn itself started to come out of the closet.

Leading the charge was Chi Chi LaRue, who was rocketing to the top of the industry in record time, a hail of sequins swirling behind him. He had graduated to the big leagues, becoming a member of Catalina's stable and eventually going on to work for Falcon as well. But more important, he brought a new mood to the industry, making what was once a group of individual companies toiling in self-imposed anonymity in the San Fernando Valley into a sort of festive—and very public—nonstop party. "No one had come along to glamorize porn stars before Chi Chi," says Kinnick. "Chi Chi would go out five nights a week, with an entourage, sweeping into a bar with her porn stars in tow and a drag queen or two. They were looked at and talked about and photographed." New-school drag had hit its stride, and Gender and LaRue and Karen Dior were its chief L.A. avatars. Individually and together they were in demand at gay clubs across the fashionable spectrum, from the big West Hollywood discos to underground once-a-week clubs like Sit & Spin and Trade. (Stefano himself made his drag debut, under the uninspired named of Josephine Stefano, in an elaborate show at Sit & Spin. "He was an ugly woman," Karen Dior remembers; it was Josephine's swan song too.) The trio decorated the rock band the Johnny Depp Clones, who played at both gay clubs and more traditional rock venues. And because they all worked in the gay porn industry, they traveled with an ever-changing cast of porn starlets, of whom Stefano was the chief and most consistent example. Along with Sharon Kane, who was becoming the business's unofficial female mascot, they made up a gay porn brat pack, as Gender put it. The fashionability of drag enhanced the image of the porn biz, gussying up its previously seedy reputation.

"Suddenly it was vaguely fashionable to be an out-and-about porn star, to be seen in public, to be photographed in the local gay press," says Kinnick. "Not only was it not fashionable before '89—it was unheard of.

"A Matt Sterling or a John Travis or a William Higgins or a Chuck Holmes were all from the old school. They were extremely discreet, unseen, invisible," Kinnick adds. "Probably because in the '70s, when they began, porn was close enough to the edge of legality that the last thing you wanted to do was go out in public and be photographed."

But LaRue was both a member of a new generation and a man cut from very different cloth than his gay porn forebears. Roughly twenty years younger than the elder generation, he grew up at a time when attitudes toward homosexuality were beginning to thaw. When at long last in 1974 the American Psychiatric Association removed homosexuality from its official *Diagnostic and Statistic Manual of Mental Disorders,* LaRue was fourteen years old. Higgins and Holmes & Co. were grown men.

As a drag performer he'd actively sought the limelight, and he saw no reason to act differently in his porn directing career. The two careers, in fact, fed each other, and his openness worked to his advantage in the business. "A lot of directors in the gay porn business don't want people to know who they are," says LaRue. "And I was screaming, 'Look at me! I'm fabulous! I'm Chi Chi LaRue! I'm a big drag queen! I'm a big porn director!' It helped attract talent, and it still does." As the most public face of the gay porn scene, LaRue would be the person young men were directed to when they expressed a yen for getting into the business.

As the industry's hottest new star—and, conveniently, a bottom—it was perhaps inevitable that Stefano would be teamed with Jeff Stryker, the most established. Stryker had started his own production company and cast Stefano and Matt Gunther for the finale of *On the Rocks.* Stefano received second billing. The Stryker straight-man mystique had become such an industry legend that it was worked into the video itself. Stryker plays himself, a role regrettably beyond his acting capabilities, but his almost tediously flawless body is displayed to good effect. The final scene is set in a gym. Gunther plays a porn star wanna-be who is chatting up Stefano when Stryker walks in. Stryker offers to help Gunther with his bench presses; with the immortal Stryker equipment more or less astride his face, Gunther is soon distracted. Stefano then walks up and asks Stryker, apropos of nothing, "So why don't you ever kiss guys in films?" Stryker remedies the situation with a fleeting French kiss, and the scene winds on in the traditional manner.

It's not a moment that will go down in cinema history, but the Stryker-Stefano kiss was an acknowledgment that the business had changed. To maintain the goodwill of the audience, Stryker obviously felt it necessary to dispel the notion—a notion that had previously been his selling point—that he was fundamentally averse to true intimacy with men. That Stefano was the man to receive the kiss was appropriate, since it was his ascension to stardom that had signaled the end of the exclusively "straight" superstar era.

CHAPTER SIX

If Stefano spent a significant portion of 1990 posing or performing for the camera, he spent a good part of the rest of it in a state of chemically induced euphoria. At the beginning of the year he was still living with Doug Smith in the Confetti Apartments, in an odd ménage supported by Stefano's sex income and Smith's drug proceeds. It was a blithely alternative universe, in which arguments about drugs did not revolve around whether or not to take them but which ones to take. Stefano had been smoking crack before he and Smith moved in together, and Smith disapproved—it was too down-market, too harsh. The conflict brought Stefano to tears. "Why is it OK for you to do what you do?" Smith remembers him asking. "If you like me as a person, why do you judge me?" Smith the crystal dealer didn't have an answer to that one. But he was on firmer ground when he objected to Stefano's smoking angel dust in their apartment:

He hated the smell. He also knew it was dangerous, expensive, and difficult to obtain—Stefano was having it sent in bundles from Philadelphia. It was also rather outré: West Hollywood boys did not do angel dust—it didn't go with the lifestyle that Smith was rigidly pursuing. You had to wear the right clothes, subscribe to the right magazines, do the right drugs. Crystal, for instance, was very much the right drug, but Stefano didn't like it. And Smith had a friend who was selling a newly fashionable substance, the animal tranquilizer ketamine, with the cute street name of Special K. Its effects were similar to those of angel dust: It was a dissociative drug—it put you out.

Smith campaigned to get Stefano to switch from PCP to Special K, which had the putative advantages of being less toxic, less expensive, and more readily available. "I told him, 'If you do it, I promise you'll never do PCP again,'" Smith says. "I think I begged him until he gave in." Special K would become Stefano's drug of choice for the next few years, although he had passing fondnesses for other substances.

Was the drug use a symptom of Stefano's deep discomfort with his new career, a means of escape from a manner of life he found degrading and shameful? Decidedly not, at least in the beginning, say all who worked with him on his early films. He was a young man who had found his niche, who loved sex and was almost deliriously happy to be getting paid for it.

On the set of the early LaRue film *Karen's Bi-Line*—Sabin's living room, as it happened—Stefano was interviewed in between scenes by Mickey Skee, a writer who covers the industry and who would become part of the porn brat pack. At the time he was relatively new to the industry and was somewhat startled by the unorthodox forum of the conversation. "He was the first person I'd interviewed naked," Skee recalls, adding abruptly, "*he* was naked, not me." Stefano walked into Skee's room (he was living in the house where the shoot was taking place) in a state of visible arousal and remained erect for the entirety of the interview—indeed for the duration of the shoot. "He had a boner for four hours," Skee says. "It never went down. It was a little unnerving. His comment was, 'I'm always horny. There's good-looking guys around; I'm naked.'" His physical excitement was matched by his enthusiasm for his new line of work. He talked a blue streak, if you will, about his plans for the business, rattling off names of partners he hoped to work with or speaking of those he had worked with in a tone of childlike awe. He didn't consider porn stars celebrities of a lesser order; to him, they were as big as Hollywood's biggest. "Have you ever met anyone that you idolize, and were you in awe of them at first?" Skee remembers asking. Stefano answered, "I'm friends with Jon Vincent now—and Sharon Kane. It's like a dream come true. I told her last night it was a fantasy come true. I really enjoy what I do." Speaking to *Manshots* magazine shortly after entering the business, Stefano reiterated his enthusiasm for his work, saying, "I always wanted to get into porno. When I was a young kid, I used to watch it and would fantasize about being with that person, especially people I liked. It always made me feel alive. I always wanted to do it, and I can't believe that today I am doing it. I love the business. I really do. I think it's exciting, something I want to do, something I don't feel bad about doing... Because I like sex, and when I'm on the set, I don't care who's there watching—we're going to have a good time. It's not all work to me. It's one of my fantasies that I'm acting out."

Far from feeling exploited, Stefano felt in the beginning that working in the video business gave him a freedom that he would not have had if he had taken advantage of some of the offers of more personal support that had come his way.

"When I first came out here, I had so many opportunities: 'Don't do movies, be with me,'" he told *Manshots*. "I don't want to be taken care of, I want to do it on my own. I don't want a rich 'daddy' to support me. I don't want to be with somebody I don't want to be with. I'd rather go hustle on the boulevard."

Unlike many porn performers who enter the business solely to make money and cover any qualms they may have about the job with a businesslike air, Stefano didn't take his work seriously—it was too much fun. He'd wander off the set if he got bored, heedless of the elaborate maneuvers sometimes necessary to bring his partner to a state of readiness. "He was a little bit bratty," recalls Karen Dior. "He was like a little kid; he enjoyed all the attention and would be wasting time. Larry would say, 'OK, we're going to shoot now. Here we go. Stay on the set, please.'" He treated shooting a scene almost as if it were a first date. Girl talk with Gender during makeup would be a whispered colloquy about Stefano's partner. "The first thing he would always talk about was the guy," Gender says. "I'd start by saying, 'Oh, he's cute.' He'd say, 'Really? You think so?' After we'd played that for a while, I'd say, 'He really likes you.' He'd say, *Really?* He was so naive, so sincere about being happy."

But, of course, the downside to Stefano's inability to see his job in a professional light was that he felt no obligation to perform if he didn't happen to find his assigned partner palatable. "He was tailor-made for the industry in that he had no qualms about the social stigma of being in the industry," says Gender, "but if he didn't like someone sexually, we'd know it, and Larry would find out, and we'd have to find someone else. A true professional would perform anyway."

He wasn't particularly interested in the moviemaking process, seeming to see it as a nuisance that got in the way of sex. LaRue got a call from the set of *Idol Eyes,* which was one of Stefano's first big-budget films. Stefano didn't particularly care about the importance of the video to his career: He was bored and couldn't believe the trouble the producers were taking to film a sex scene. "I'm still here," he said to LaRue, pouting, "and I've been here for three days."

But it wasn't surprising that Stefano had trouble distinguishing work from play: The line between was often blurred for the small coterie of players in LaRue and Stefano's circle. A day on the set would more often than not be followed by a night out at a club or a party, and sex was just as much a part of the after-hours activity as it was an on-set necessity. They were young and attractive and shared a freewheeling libidinousness that was enhanced by the mind-altering substances at their disposal. For the gay porn brat pack, the war on drugs was being fought on another front; the age of AIDS was happening on another planet.

Stefano had been chosen by an organization called the Fans of X-Rated Films as best gay newcomer of the year. LaRue, Dior, Gender, and Stefano all piled into the back of a limousine on Valentine's Day to attend the award ceremony, being held on the Santa Monica Pier. They made the most of the limousine, which was a novelty, and drank champagne on the way. The fire marshal had insisted that the space heaters set up on the pier be turned off, so alcohol was required to keep spirits up. LaRue and Stefano were scheduled to entertain— LaRue singing, Stefano and another boy dancing—and by the time they hit the stage, they had reached a state that made public performance a cagey proposition. Stefano didn't have too much trouble: He and his partner began simulating various acts of copulation, making even the fans of X-rated video a little uneasy—it was a predominantly heterosexual crowd.

LaRue managed to put over his number but destroyed the podium in the process ("I think she sat on it," recalls Dior). No matter; the gang was ready to make an exit anyway. They piled back into the limo, having picked up Kane and a couple of extra boys, and headed back to Hollywood. LaRue played hostess en route, passing out the cocaine with a liberal if somewhat unsteady hand.

Back at the Porn Palace, the group piled out of the limo and bounded upstairs. LaRue accidentally sneezed the rest of the cocaine all over the bedspread, to general consternation. Happily, it was a black bedspread, and all was not lost. Things began getting sexual soon after the drugs ran out, when LaRue turned to the only anatomical female present and said, "Sharon Kane, I wanna eat your pussy!" It wasn't unusual for LaRue to be directing sex, certainly, but this was a novelty. "I've never eaten pussy before, and I wanna eat your pussy," he said by way of explanation. Kane—who was by no means averse to initiating gay men into the rites of heterosex— couldn't object and indeed helped LaRue along, as the rest of the party watched in fascination. It was better than a video and infinitely more spontaneous. "There we were, watching Chi Chi, in full drag, giving head to Sharon, with Sharon coaching," marvels Dior. If Fellini had made X-rated movies, he might have conjured up something equally outlandish, but he couldn't have topped it. The evening ended on an equally comic note, as all scrambled to get together enough money to pay for the limo that LaRue had left waiting downstairs; he had expected to pop in for only a minute.

The occasional orgy was by no means Stefano's only extracurricular sexual activity. He became enamored of a man named Sal, one of the West Hollywood Showgirls Smith was running with. More beautiful even than Stefano, with classically chiseled features and an ego to match, Sal was not an ideal choice, particularly since he already had a boyfriend. And while video viewers across the country were coupling in their imaginations with Stefano, Sal was only mildly interested. He slept with him but also denigrated him for his career in porn. He borrowed money, which Stefano freely lent without worrying that he'd get it back. There was no danger, however, of being looked down upon by another man Stefano dated briefly, fellow porn star Rod Phillips. "Nick was in love with him," says Smith, "and it was sexually incredible for a couple of months." But the relationship fizzled, although they remained in touch.

"He didn't have steady boyfriends. He was always in love with someone new," says Dior, who had also joined the ranks in the Porn Palace. "I was jealous of him, and he was jealous of me. I got attention from all these big straight guys who liked me in drag, and I wasn't interested. He liked all the guys who liked me, while I liked the guys who liked him."

And there were plenty of guys who liked him—for a night, anyway. Fame comes quickly in the porn business. People had dutifully lined up for Stefano's autograph at a Las Vegas trade show before they knew who he was. ("It's the only industry where you can become a star before doing a movie," Gender quips.) Stefano had performed in a lot of movies and appeared on a lot of magazine covers in a short period of time, and he became a recognizable face in the West Hollywood clubs and bars, where he spent his nights out. But his looks had always gained him attention, and he didn't seem to be unduly swayed by his new notoriety. "The funny thing is, he didn't notice if the whole club was looking at him," says Gender. "If one guy was looking at him, he was just as excited as if a whole club was. And I was always delightfully surprised by the fact that he was always attracted to a person who he thought was attracted to him for more than being Joey Stefano."

But being Joey Stefano clearly had its advantages. With a quickly growing stack of videos behind him, Stefano's name had gained marquee value. He had gone from making $500 per scene in his first videos, and appearing in only one scene, to making $1,500 per scene—the upper end of the scale—in record time. Still, more money can be made dancing, either partly or totally nude, depending on the venue, and as soon as Stefano's name was established, he became a dancer in demand at gay discos and strip clubs across the country. Between his videos and his dancing gigs, Stefano was bringing in several thousand dollars a month, more money than he'd ever seen before in his life. He frittered away much of it on drugs and clothes and treating friends to evenings on the town, but he also pined for a traditional symbol of middle-class respectability: a house. "It was his dream to live in a house," says Smith. More than respectability, perhaps, a house to Stefano meant security. He had lived on the streets, in seedy hotels, in a series of apartments, and all seemed to reinforce the transitory nature of his life; a house would mean permanence, a return to the stability he associated with the years before his father's death.

And as it happened, Smith's crystal connection had evaporated, leaving him with no means of support and no way to pay his half of the rent. Fortunately, Dior, who lived just a floor away in the Confetti Apartments, had become a porn star(let) in his own right and was bringing in steady cash. Stefano proposed that they move in together, and they found a spacious three-bedroom, three-bathroom house on Sierra Bonita Avenue, several blocks west of the Confetti Apartments, and located in the more desirable West Hollywood. Dior didn't have enough money initially to put down his share of the first and last month's rent, but Stefano went ahead and paid his share too. It was both a natural act of generosity and an indication of how much the new digs could mean to him. Another sign that he wanted to start off life in his new house on a new footing was his decision to leave most of his furnishings in the apartment; Smith was astonished that he took only his black faux-leather furniture with him. "Time to go— we'll buy new things" was his attitude, Smith remembers. The move west was a move upward on the fashionability scale; left behind in Hollywood was Stefano's queen-size waterbed, not quite the thing in the city's tonier western parts.

But once ensconced in the palatial new home, Stefano continued to pursue the hedonistic lifestyle to which he'd become accustomed—or addicted. The black furniture was stranded in the middle of the spacious living room. It never gained much company. The boys lived in their bedrooms, and trash steadily piled up in the other rooms. ("We never cleaned," Dior recalls flatly.) The fabulously appointed kitchen went virtually unused most of the time. Stefano had no car, no concerns about money, and simple taste in food. He'd call up Pink Dot, a market chain that delivers basic foodstuffs, and order the Stefano staples: Wonder bread, peanut butter and jelly, Häagen-Dazs ice cream, and a carton of cigarettes.

"He was going out of town a lot, and whenever he got back he'd call Pink Dot and have them deliver the same things," says Dior. "Of course, he always forgot that he already had a lot of Wonder bread and Häagen-Dazs ice cream. So we'd have nine loaves of Wonder bread in the kitchen, peanut butter and jelly for days, and nothing else."

It was a diet to make nutritionists *plotz,* but Stefano, to the eternal wonder of his friends, always looked beautiful. He seemed to thrive on junk food ("The more sugar he ate, the better he looked," recalls Dior). His chief dietary supplements continued to be controlled substances, which also seemed to have no detrimental effects on his appearance.

Ecstasy, an amphetaminelike drug also known as MDMA, had become the rage among young gay men—indeed, among young men and women of all sexual stripes who moved in circles where mild or not so mild drug use was taken for granted as a social stimulant. It was one of the breed of "designer drugs" manufactured by replicating the psychoactive properties of a drug while altering the molecular structure to avoid prosecution under the Controlled Substances Act. (Although in 1986 the Analogs Act was passed, making such drugs also illegal, they remained widely available, probably because they are easy to manufacture. A minimal investment in good lab equipment can produce street drugs worth millions of dollars.) Ecstasy was originally created in the early twentieth century as an appetite suppressant and comes in tablet form, selling for about $20 a pill. It provides a euphoric high that can last for a couple of hours, characterized by both a heightened sense of self and a feeling of connection with other people; communication becomes imperative. According to authors Richard G. Schlaadt and Peter T. Shannon in their 1993 book *Drugs: Use, Misuse, and Abuse,* its side effects, however, aren't known; studies in animals have revealed brain cell damage, and it's likely to have the same effects on humans.

Its side effects were of no interest to Stefano and his circle, and he did a lot of communicating while under its effects that spring. Dior recalls a particularly "Ecstatic" trip to Palm Springs. Stefano had been working hard and making a lot of money and wanted to get away for a weekend. Dior was temporarily without funds, so Stefano sprang for the trip. They drove into town with a pile of Ecstasy at hand ("Nick would go and buy one hundred hits of Ecstasy at a time," Dior says), and spent the weekend making friends. Dior took three hits of Ecstasy before they went out Friday night; Stefano probably took more. They hit a gay club, Daddy Warbucks, where Stefano was instantly recognized. Back at the hotel, they slept with "various people," Dior recalls. The next day was spent lying by the pool. "Every hour he would feed me Ecstasy," Dior says. "I remember being very happy. When we left on Sunday, the owner of the hotel came out and personally thanked us for coming, and no wonder—we had slept with everybody there."

Karen Dior was working almost as much as Stefano was. He had begun his porn career performing in drag but had since diversified into more traditional roles. For his first two movies, *Sharon and Karen* and *Karen's Bi-Line*—both directed by LaRue and costarring Stefano and Sharon Kane—he had made $500 a scene. Although not blockbusters by any yardstick, the videos had made a sensation, creating a small new genre of porn. "This whole concept of mixing genders in porn was something new," says Dave Kinnick. "There had been bi movies, of course, but they were always squeaky-clean. No one had crossed gender lines before like Chi Chi had, where suddenly cute boys are dressed up like drag queens, pulling out these big dicks. And then there's a pussy in the middle of this gay porn movie. One scene has a real woman, and the next has two women who aren't real women; it was confusing, but it was fresh." And it shook up the market. For his third movie, *Painted,* Dior's fee was doubled, to $1,000 a scene for three scenes. He was performing out of drag in movies for LaRue and others as Ricky Van and was such a dependable performer that LaRue would call on his services as a "stunt dick," as it was called, when a slated performer had trouble delivering the goods at the last minute; many a close-up in LaRue's early oeuvre was not an anatomical match with the performers in the scene. Viewers besotted with the exaggerated machismo of a porn star would be surprised to know that some of the genitalia on display belonged to one of L.A.'s premier drag queens.

With drag an increasingly hot draw at gay bars and nudity an eternal one, it was only natural to combine the two for financial purposes. The gay porn brat pack began hitting the road in various permutations to perform at gay bars all over the country. LaRue or Dior or Gender would host and belt out a few tunes, while Stefano and any number of other boys would strip. They packed the house and made money both in fees and tips. The tours would be organized by an agent with varying degrees of efficiency. Dior describes a typical tour, in this case with Stefano, Tony Davis, and Andrew Michaels:

"It started off badly. The organizer was supposed to send us cash before we left, but he didn't send as much as he said he would. We went to Minneapolis anyway, for a week at the Gay '90s, where Chi Chi met us. Half the plane tickets were screwed up, so the club owners would have to buy us extra tickets. But anyway, we missed almost every single plane. I was like the den mother, and Tony, Andrew, and Joey were like little kids. Everywhere we went, I'd have to say, 'Come on, we've got to pack. We've got to catch a plane now. Come on!' And everybody would take forever, because we'd been out all night the night before, of course."

The less-than-respectable nature of some of the establishments they had to perform in was vividly illustrated in one city. "We were supposed to get half of our fees up front and half after the show," continues Dior. "But at this one club, we got there and they said the manager wasn't there. We started getting ready anyway. As show time approached, the manager still wasn't there. I was getting worried, but they promised us the manager would be there by the end of the show.

"We were all wrapped up in being stars, with people clamoring to see us: 'The show must go on!' So we went on, and after the show they called us into the office. There were two big Guidos standing there. They said, 'I'm sure you've figured out by now that we're not going to pay you. You can just get your stuff and leave, and if you try not to, we'll kill you.'

"We left."

Each of the boys had his own fans, but Stefano was the biggest name, and occasionally he would let the others know he knew it. "He certainly felt like he was the star, and at times he had no consideration for anyone else," Dior says. "He could be charming or a total brat. He got away with it a lot because he could. People would do what he wanted. If he was on a set and he wanted that person to walk over there, it was easier to get that person to do it than to have Joey walk off the set. I wouldn't let him get away with it. I'd say, 'I'm not one of your fans. You can jolly well go get your own cocktail.'"

Although he wasn't partying any more than any of the other tour members, his compulsiveness came through in other ways. "At one hotel we went to check out, and when they went to print out our bills, out came reams and reams of pages of phone calls," Dior says. "Joey had spent, like, $200 on 976 calls—in one night. It was too freaky. This was Joey Stefano, whom every man at these clubs we're performing at wants, yet he spends $200 in a single night calling 976 numbers."

It wasn't the only sign that there was a deep reservoir of emptiness in Joey Stefano that no amount of public adoration, no abundance of drugs, no sufficiency of sex could assuage. When he was not in a state of chemically or sexually induced euphoria, Stefano struggled with demons that he could rarely bring himself to talk about. "He was really miserable," remembers Dior. "He came home one night from somewhere, and he was going to be leaving again the next day, and I saw him sitting on the front porch crying. I went out and tried to hold him and comfort him, but he just wouldn't talk about it. He never talked about how he was feeling; he talked about what he did, where he'd been, the drugs he'd bought, but he couldn't really connect with people, couldn't seem to communicate." Dior sat with him for a while, hoping he would open up, but he didn't. Later Stefano went out and dulled the pain the only way he knew how: by dosing himself with drugs.

Indeed, there was a crucial difference between the manner in which Stefano took drugs and that of most of his friends. For LaRue, Dior, Kane, and most of the porn pack he associated with, drug-taking was a recreational activity. It was a way of making a night out at a club more lively, a weekend more wild, a performance more fabulous. They were consistent but casual users, like thousands of other people their age. As LaRue puts it, "I've done my share of drugs, but I'm the person who has to wake up on Monday morning and get everything together. I do, and I have for the ten years I've been in this business." But for Stefano, drugs filled a deeper need; they were his way of coping with everyday life. He took drugs the way other people put on sunglasses when they go outdoors: as an automatic reflex. (Shortly before his death, Mickey Skee asked him, after he'd said he'd been sober all day, "Does it bother you?" Stefano's answer: "Yeah, it does.")

In their book *Drugs: Use, Misuse, and Abuse,* Schlaadt and Shannon synthesized research on factors behind drug use and gave a general psychological portrait of the typical drug-dependent personality:

People inclined toward drug use usually suffer from psychological tensions that, left unabated, become painful and may produce a state of helplessness. Such a state may bring on self-deprecation and depression, exacerbating the problem and contributing to further tension and loss of self-esteem. This cycle of negativism may result in the use of psychoactive substances and, depending on the intensity of the predependent state, drug dependence. The gratifying use of narcotics relieves the tension and may be tantamount to a return to the womb, where frustrations are nonexistent and the painful realities of existence have little impact.

Generally speaking, the personality traits of a drug abuser may include (1) difficulty handling frustration, anxiety and depression; (2) an urge for immediate gratification of desires; (3) difficulty relating with others; (4) low self-esteem; (5) impulsiveness, risk taking and little regard for health; and (6) resistance to authority.

It's a startlingly precise picture of Nick Iacona.

The extent of Stefano's dependence on drugs—and the havoc it wrought on his life—began to become apparent when Dior and Kane eased up on their recreational use. They started attending the popular Course in Miracles self-help lectures given by Marianne Williamson. The series was phenomenally popular, particularly among young gay men, in the early '90s. A tepid blend of New Age pop psychology and vague spirituality, the course was something of a social necessity among the young and fashionable. Dior and Kane would gather together a gaggle of porn stars and sweep into the lecture halls each week, and for a while Stefano came along, seeming to evince a certain amount of interest. But it didn't last. "He was lazy," says Dior. "He wasn't willing to or didn't know how to do the work; everything had been handed to him." Nor did he admit the necessity for a course in self-improvement. "He didn't know how to say, 'I need help.' I would try to talk to him, but he never acknowledged that he had a problem; he didn't even really say that he was un-happy."

But it was clear that the drugs were both masking and exac-erbating an underlying unease. During the summer Dior came down with pneumonia; he returned home with news of the diagnosis to a climate-controlled house whose thermostat was set at a chilly 45 degrees. When Stefano was coming down from a drug binge, he'd sweat a lot, so he would turn down the thermostat to minimize his discomfort. Says Dior: "I went ahead and changed it and went in to tell him that I had, say-ing, 'Honey, the thermostat was on 45—that's kind of low. I just went to the doctor, and I'm really sick; I need it to be a little bit warmer.' " Stefano flew out of his room and into a rage, punching a hole in the wall. "He was screaming that he was going to set it at whatever he wanted to," Dior continues. "I was scared of him—I'd never seen him like that. So I left the house."

Thinking Dior had gone down the street to Sharon Kane's, Stefano called her in a rage; she didn't know what he was talking about. When Dior returned the next day, he tried to talk to Stefano about it, but he wouldn't even acknowledge the hole in the wall. "He wouldn't talk about what happened," says Dior, "but I knew it wasn't just about the thermostat."

The tantrum was a shock, but just as difficult to live with was the general air of chaos that had taken over the house. "I would come home and be getting ready to go to bed, and I'd knock on his door, and there would be twenty people in his room, sitting around really high," says Dior. "When he was gone there would be no one there; when he was there the place would be full. He would take these strays in off the street; he'd say, 'This is so-and-so, and they're going to be staying with us for a while.' "

Stefano's generosity was always remarkable, but his indifference to money was a double-edged sword for Dior, who had to worry about paying the rent because Stefano didn't pay attention to such matters. "Since money meant nothing to him, if he couldn't pay the rent, that meant nothing to him either," says Dior. "I'd be screaming for him to pay the rent, and then he'd leave town for a while. We'd be about to be evicted, and then he'd come back to town with thousands of dollars, and we'd pay off months of back rent."

There was no dramatic denouement, but it was clear that the household was an uncomfortable place for both Dior and Stefano. Since Stefano was spending more and more time on the road dancing, it seemed natural for him to move out. He packed up his clothes and moved in with Kane for a few weeks before moving on to San Francisco. It was fall of 1990. The circle of friends that had formed during the making of *Sharon and Karen* was beginning to disband. For a while they had functioned as an unorthodox kind of family, with all the attendant closeness and conflict that that engendered. It was only after Stefano left the supportive intimacy of the Porn Pack behind that it would become apparent just how much he needed it to maintain his equilibrium in the emotionally draining lifestyle he'd begun to pursue.

CHAPTER SEVEN

There is no such thing as a gay movie star. For purposes of press releases, TV interviews, magazine spreads, and talk shows, they are all steadfast heterosexuals. That gay men and women hunger for a movie icon they can claim as their own is amply demonstrated by the persistence of rumors of stars' homosexuality that spread through the gay population. Name a movie star—any movie star—and you can find someone who has heard, from the most unimpeachable sources, mind you, that he or she is gay. Tom Cruise? The marriage is a sham. John Travolta? Ditto. Tom Selleck? Please—the mustache! Jodie Foster? Where have you been?

It's a process that begins almost simultaneously with an actor's rise to a certain level of prominence. George Clooney's first movie after his fame had been established on television's *ER* had been out just one day before stories were being spread that, yes, he too is one of ours. Certainly it is true that some of the avowedly heterosexual movie stars are in fact gay, but the promiscuity of the rumor mill speaks to a deeper issue. Gay people need to believe some movie stars are gay—any movie stars—because it validates their significance to American culture. The culture of celebrity, like it or not, has more and more become the only culture all Americans share. Black or white, straight or gay, CEO or CPA or sanitation worker, everyone tuned in to the O.J. Simpson murder trial, and it wasn't because of the racial issues involved or the horrific nature of the crime. It was because Simpson is a very famous man. So the absence of any openly gay men and women among the most famous of the famous, movie stars, is an unsettling idea to the homosexual community. It says that at America's apex, among the gods and goddesses, gay people are not welcome; gay people are not allowed to breathe the rarefied air that circulates in the upper reaches of celebrity. They are not allowed to exist.

Porn stars, on a literal level, are thus the only gay movie stars. (How sad an irony it is, therefore, that many of the biggest make public their private heterosexuality!) It is one reason that they are accorded more attention—and a smattering of respect—among the gay community than straight porn stars are in heterosexual culture. No straight fashion designer would think of featuring a porn star in a runway show, as Thierry Mugler did with Jeff Stryker. No straight-porn award show would be likely to find judges among the straight community of the caliber that the Fourth Annual Gay Erotic Video Awards found among gay men: filmmaker John Waters, Oscar-winning director John Schlesinger, film-music composer and Oscar nominee Marc Shaiman (*A Few Good Men, Broadcast News, The American President*). The host was Bruce Vilanch, who writes comic material for a number of stars and regularly contributes to the Oscar show. Jeff Stryker, Ryan Idol, and the many other top gay porn stars are a big draw at gay discos not just because they are sexy; there are gay men of equal beauty to be found in the discos themselves, probably. It's because they are famous, and in America in the twentieth century, fame inevitably brings a residue of respect.

But it's not just their fame that gives porn stars a significant presence in the gay community. They are not celebrated despite their occupation, as the closest thing to real movie stars, but because of it. Straight men and women arrive at adulthood with a large store of romantic and/or sexual imagery to draw upon in forging relationships. They've been inundated since birth with pictures of the age-old story of boy meets girl. From *Snow White* and *Cinderella* to *Gone With the Wind* to *Last Tango in Paris* to *The Bridges of Madison County,* movies have provided an informal but vital education in the way women and men relate to each other sexually and socially. But there is no gay *Cinderella,* no gay *Gone With the Wind,* no gay *The Way We Were* (well, perhaps *The Way We Were* is the gay *The Way We Were,* but let it pass). Gay men and women have to come to terms with their desires in a cinematic void, without a fund of visual imagery to point the way, to affirm the importance of their sexual natures as romantic movies do for heterosexuals. (There have, of course, been a few films depicting gay romances over the years, particularly recently, but they can practically be counted on one hand.) So gay men have to find visual representations of men relating sexually to each other the only place it is to be found: in pornography. For many a gay man, stumbling upon a gay porn magazine may be the first concrete indication that there are others like him out there. Renting a gay porn movie or going to a theater to see one may be the first time many gay men see acted out the images that invaded their imaginations when puberty struck. It's the first evidence they have that the couplings they long for actually do take place. So gay porn has deeper cultural resonance than its straight equivalent. It is, of course, on a conscious level created and used for sexual stimulation, but it has a deeper significance too. "Pornography makes gay men visible," writes John Burger in *One-Handed Histories.* "It is an attempt by gay men to rewrite themselves into American history." Richard Dyer, in the article "Male Gay Porn: Coming to Terms" in *Jump Cut* magazine, puts it simply, saying that porn "has made life bearable for millions of gay men."

It's not likely that Joey Stefano ever thought of his career in porn as a social crusade. He was, if anything, anticerebral: He spent a good portion of his life taking drugs precisely to avoid thinking. Perhaps if it had been brought to his attention that his career was of cultural significance to gay men, he might have had some armor against the contravening—and vastly more widely held—belief that it is a sleazy, degrading way to make a living. But in truth most workers in the adult-film industry give no thought to any larger significance their work might have, and it shows in the product they produce. The vast majority of gay porn doesn't leave the viewer much to think about, unless it is to marvel at the paucity of wit, style, and intelligence on display; to ponder the sometimes awe-inspiring inability of the performers to deliver simple dialogue with a shred of credibility; to wonder at the filmmakers' ability to find ugly couches.

A rare exception is the work of Jerry Douglas, who directed Stefano in the 1991 release *More of a Man,* by most accounts Stefano's finest film. Douglas came to the industry through the legitimate theater. He graduated from Yale Drama School in the late '60s and toiled in New York's burgeoning off-Broadway theater scene for the next few years, writing and directing plays that failed to make a significant splash. With the sexual revolution percolating along, nudity had become fashionable on New York stages, and in 1970 Douglas was approached to direct one of the first to capitalize on the new mood, a play called *Score.* (It featured a young Sylvester Stallone: "I gave him his SAG card," recalls Douglas.) The play was a modest hit and was optioned by Radley Metzger, one of the era's two titans of soft-core pornography (the other being Russ Meyer). Metzger hired Douglas to script the movie, and Douglas learned the moviemaking process during the film's Yugoslavia shoot.

His theatrical career hadn't taken off, so when Douglas was asked to do a hard-core gay film in 1972, he gave it a shot. He had become friendly with gay porn star Casey Donovan, who had been in some of Douglas's off-Broadway shows, and featured Donovan and George Payne in *The Back Row.* The film was a notable success, running at New York's 55th Street Theater longer than any other adult film up to that time, but Douglas made little money. It was the same story with his next movie, a bisexual flick, *Both Ways,* starring Andrea True and Darby Lloyd Rains. "I never saw a penny," says Douglas, "so I said, 'That's it—fuck it.' The film industry in those days was much more sleazy, much more Mob-infiltrated; certainly the gay industry was run by straight people."

True to his word, Douglas spent the next 18 years as a dispassionate observer of the porn scene. He worked as a journalist, wrote a few books, and eventually established himself in the print arm of the gay porn industry, becoming executive editor of FirstHand publications, which publishes gay porn fiction and skin magazines. In 1988 he founded the colorfully titled *Manshots* magazine, which focuses on the video industry. His first issue featured an interview with All Worlds

Video president Rick Ford. A friendship grew, and Ford began asking Douglas to take up the camera again.

"One day I was feeling very piss-elegant," Douglas relates, "and I said, 'All right, I'll make a movie, but you've got to give me final cut, royalties—which is unheard of—and you've got to give me Tim Lowe.' " Lowe was one of the hottest names in the business at the time. "A week later Rick called back and said, 'It's a deal.' I had no choice."

In the summer of 1989 Douglas shot *Fratrimony,* his first movie in some sixteen years. The video was a critical and commercial success: Lowe won best actor at the Adult Video News Awards, the Oscars of the porn industry, sponsored by the business's primary trade paper. The film was nominated for best picture. Douglas's filmmaking career was re-launched. In fact, it was at the AVN awards show itself, watching Chi Chi LaRue perform in drag for the first time, that Douglas got the idea for his next movie, which would be *More of a Man.*

"I was overwhelmed by his performance," remembers Douglas. "But you don't write a porn movie for a drag queen. We decided to make a movie together, at any rate. About this time, Larry discovered Nick. He was raving about this wonderful blue-collar kid from Philadelphia." Douglas, who lives and works in New York, had dinner with LaRue and Stefano during a trip to L.A., and watching the interaction between the two gave him the kernel that would become the movie. He was impressed by the strange mixture of Stefano's personality.

"Nick was a street kid," Douglas says, "but like the best of Hollywood street kids, he had an element of class about him that transcended the rough edges of the street kid. Joey could look as good in a tuxedo as he could crawling around the floor of a back room naked. He had the same kind of inviting hostility that characterized Marlon Brando, James Dean, Steve

McQueen; Joey was very much a rebel. That first night he was gracious, monosyllabic, friendly, and hostile—all at the same time. He was disinterested and fascinated; he was a bundle of paradoxes. Nick wanted to be a porn star more than anything in the world; it was transparently obvious that he had found his niche."

Douglas was amused by LaRue's mother-hen behavior around Stefano and could tell that LaRue was in love with him. He also knew that Stefano was the sensation of the year and that LaRue had proprietary rights. "I owe a lot in my career to Larry," Douglas admits. "Larry is a very generous man, and the most generous thing he ever did was hand me the hottest star in the industry for *More of a Man,* after I had done only one movie." He went back to New York and penned the video's 55-page script—fifty-five pages longer than the average porn film's script—then returned to California to shoot.

The movie is a coming-of-age story starring Stefano as a construction worker named Vito who's plagued by Catholic guilt and in denial about his sexuality, even as he haunts glory holes. LaRue plays Vito's best friend Belle Zahringen (get it?), who works in a bar and sings at clubs. That Stefano wasn't used to the notion of actually portraying a character other than himself—despite, or perhaps because of, the dozens of movies he had done—became clear early on. "Nick didn't know a great deal about acting or about the concept of theater or film or characterization," says Douglas. "I like to think that I taught him something about that. One of the first things I do with an actor, whether it's a stage play or a fuck film, is take the actor aside with the script and say, 'Your first job as an actor is to read the script and say, "How is the character like me, and how is he not like me?"' It registered with Joey. He got the idea instantly. I mailed him a copy of the video of *Rocky* and told him to watch the film and steal everything he could.

"One of my most wonderful moments as a director was the day we did the first setup, subsequently cut; there was shot of him walking out of the church and walking up to his truck and kicking the tire. After it was over, Nick came over to me and put his arm around me and said, 'Did you see my Sylvester Stallone walk?'"

He was learning the rudiments of the acting craft, but Stefano was something of a tabula rasa; Douglas had to keep reiterating the idea that he was supposed to be playing a character. "One day he walked onto the set wearing tight white pedal pushers, very West Hollywood–faggot," Douglas says. "He came up to me and said, 'Aren't these terrific? Aren't I going to look hot in them?' I said, 'Yeah, Joey, you look terrific in them, but Vito wouldn't be caught dead in them!' He looked at me for a long time and said, "That's right, Vito wouldn't wear these, would he? I couldn't wear these with a hard hat!'"

Stefano wasn't the only one who had trouble adjusting to the requirements of the character he was playing. In Douglas's screenplay, LaRue's Belle spent the first half of the movie looking like a plain hausfrau, the better to show off her transformation into sequined glamour in the film's final scene. But LaRue didn't particularly like playing the frump, particularly in scenes with the man he was besotted with. "Their relationship in the movie was not so terribly different from the one I'd witnessed offscreen," explains Douglas. "They'd fight as soon as the camera stopped and then be kissing each other. Nick knew how to push Larry's buttons. One of the biggest problems on the shoot was that Larry kept saying, 'Jerry, you're making me look unattractive; I want to be beautiful.' I'd say, 'Larry, you've got the 11 o'clock number coming up; let's save some place to go.' I wanted the caterpillar turning into the butterfly. Joey wouldn't help any by walking onto the set and saying, 'Jesus, Larry, you look like shit!'"

Knowing that sexual chemistry is the key ingredient in a porn movie, Douglas consulted Stefano about whom he'd like to work with in his sex scenes. Stefano mentioned Michael Henson as someone he'd pined for since his Philadelphia days, and Douglas set about trying to find him. Like many porn performers who do a spurt of films in a short period and then drop from sight, Henson wasn't easy to find. Douglas eventually tracked him down in Sacramento and talked him into making a return to the business. Douglas was less lucky with another of Stefano's choices, the mustachioed Chad Douglas; when he couldn't find Chad, he lined up Rick Donovan, whose nickname, "Humongous," doesn't need elaboration. "Rick was fine with Joey, because Joey was something of a size queen," says Douglas.

The shoot itself was probably Stefano's longest—eight or nine days running as opposed to the "one-day wonders" that are the bread and butter of many of the smaller video companies. Stefano performed in five sex scenes as well as a few dialogue-only bits with LaRue and was on call virtually every day of the shoot. Stefano was utterly dependable once he was on the set, but getting him there was another matter. "Joey loved to play," says Douglas. "I said to him every night of the shoot, 'Honey, go home, go to sleep, don't waste it.' He would give me his certified word of honor and go right out and party all night. The only problem I had during the shoot was that I had to go up to his apartment every morning and get him out of bed; but as soon as he was up, he was all there—and it never showed on film."

The exigencies of the shoot required that Stefano be available at all times, but he wasn't always needed, so workers with free time were sometimes needed to keep him from getting into trouble. Dave Kinnick was working as a second cameraman on the shoot and offered to take him to dinner one night. He tells the story in his book *Sorry I Asked: Intimate Interviews with Gay Porn's Rank and File:*

> I was called down to San Diego to do two days of second camerawork for All Worlds Video on *More of a Man.* One of their regular cameramen had come down with the flu, and I was needed. I was present for the very intense and weird all-night shoot at the Caliph bar, in which Joey got fucked by both Chris McKenzie and Lon Flexx while thirty extras stood around and watched. We started taping that scene at 2 o'clock in the morning and finished at 7 a.m. And, for the record, Joey did get double-penetrated at one point by Lon and Chris, but we lost the shot due to lousy lighting (and being extremely punchy by that point).
>
> The following evening I asked Joey if I could take him to dinner. He agreed, and we set off in my rental car for the deli at Sixth and University. I think this following tidbit of information does more to sum up Joey's character than any sexually hair-raising story could: As I was roaming the neighborhood looking for a parking space, Joey announced that I was to find one within "a couple of blocks" of our destination. I said I'd do the best I could, but when asked why, he simply said, "I don't walk." Translation: "I'm used to people bringing me things. You'll bring it to me before I'll put myself out by walking two whole blocks."

In addition to clearing up the burning issue of that double-penetration shot, Kinnick's story gives a vivid picture of a side of Stefano that was in contrast to the generous nature he often displayed to his friends. After an acceptable parking place was found, Stefano and Kinnick did proceed to have dinner, but Stefano maintained a chilly distance. "Joey barely spoke a word the whole time," recalls Kinnick. "He didn't like speaking about his past; he didn't like speaking about his present; he didn't like speaking about his future. He would speak of men occasionally—there was a guy sitting nearby that he was eyeing. And he would answer direct questions: 'Where did you get that tattoo?' I asked. He would give me a month and a city. Then I'd ask what the significance was, and he'd stare at me like, *You must be joking. I just got it.*"

His aloofness was sometimes as startling as his sexual enthusiasm. It often seemed that the only way Stefano could connect with people was through sex. The only scene from *More of a Man* he had trouble performing in, interestingly, was a solo sequence—usually among the easiest to shoot since it involves only one performer. (Performing solo is often used as a litmus test for would-be porn performers.) "Joey couldn't get hard," says Douglas. "He'd say, 'I need someone.'" It's a fascinating snapshot of his personality. Despite the fact that he'd performed on cue in dozens of films and might have been expected to be an expert performer, being a porn star for Stefano was not primarily about money or fame or ego; it was about connecting with people through sex. When there was no one there to connect with, he simply couldn't perform. The shoot had to be canceled, the script revised. "I'll never forget that day, because he couldn't get hard," Douglas continues. "Like all stars, there was a certain amount of narcissism, but not much; Joey needed a warm body."

In contrast, Douglas recalls the final scene of the movie as the smoothest he has ever filmed. Roughly speaking, it takes three or four hours to shoot the average fifteen-minute porn sequence. "If a miracle happens, you can do it in an hour," Douglas says, "or you can wait for somebody's hard-on for twenty-four hours. But we shot the final scene in forty-five minutes. Joey couldn't wait to get at Michael." But if Stefano was charmingly eager to get to the sex, he wasn't utterly without professionalism; he had learned the elements of a porn movie and the various requirements for putting a good scene together. "My favorite outtake from *More of a Man* comes from that final scene," recounts Douglas. "Joey is lying on his back; the camera is low, behind his head; Michael Henson is just plowing him with everything he's got. Joey's into it; it's working. And all of a sudden Joey turns his head and looks smack into the camera and says, 'Jerry, are you absolutely sure you got the penetration shot?' I said, 'Yeah, I got it.' And boom—he's back into it."

The video that resulted was a hefty improvement on the average gay porn title. It concerns the gradual process of Vito's accepting his sexuality, ending with his symbolic deflowering—he'd already been deflowered a few times during the course of the story, but it's the thought that counts—inside a float at the gay pride parade. The story touches on various psychological truths about coming out, on safe sex, on activism (Vito's amour is a member of ACT UP), albeit in a sometimes dramaturgically blunt fashion. There's plenty of sex, to be sure, but it is integrated logically into the story line. And the dialogue has spark. When Belle tells Vito that Dusty, the bartender at their hangout, is going home to a boyfriend, Vito looks at her incredulously: "Nah, he's a Dodgers fan!" Though he certainly hadn't received any training and had displayed precious little acting talent in previous videos (the phrase "Fuck my ass, man!" does not admit a wide variety of interpretations, after all), Stefano acquits himself respectably. Sharon Kane does a creditable Southern accent in her turn as a hooker Vito picks up (she then turns into a man in his imagination as she services him). And LaRue gets a big musical number, the title tune, a be-gay-and-be-proud anthem that he belts out with panache. The song concludes cleverly: "I'm more of a woman than you'll ever have and more of a man than you'll ever be." Even the box cover was something of a departure: Unlike virtually all others, the men on the cover— Stefano and Henson—are actually looking at each other, rather than smoldering resolutely at the camera in an attempt to seduce browsers.

The industry took note. Exactly a year after having been inspired by LaRue's performance at the AVN Awards to write the movie, Jerry Douglas was back in Las Vegas, where *More of a Man* picked up four AVN awards: best gay video, best performer (Stefano), and best director and best screenplay for Douglas. (When Stefano accepted his award, Douglas recalls with amusement, he displayed an almost childlike forthrightness by saying, "Thanks a lot, but I would rather have won the award for best sex scene.")

The AVN show is the adult-film industry's glittering imitation of the annual rites of self-celebration indulged in by all branches of the mainstream entertainment industry. Just like the Oscars and the Emmys, it's held in a big ballroom. The men wear tuxedos, and the women wear beads and sequins. A close observer might be tipped off to the nature of the occasion by the preponderance of preternaturally enlarged breasts, for instance, but it's more or less a traditional gala affair. The list of laurels corresponds to a certain degree to categories at the Hollywood awards shows: best actor and actress, director, screenplay—with a few notable divergences, of course.

But this event is not televised to an enraptured audience of one billion viewers across the globe. And its players are not held up for universal admiration as the acknowledged apotheosis of human evolution. A movie star is not a porn star; to the world at large, a porn star is not a movie star.

Indeed, just a month later, on Valentine's Day, the video that was lauded in Las Vegas as the pinnacle of achievement in its genre was the subject of obscenity charges in Chicago. One man's award winner is another man's irredeemable trash. The confiscation of *More of a Man* at the Bijou Theater and the arrest of the theater manager prompted a quick response from the city's gay activists. The theater hired a couple of lawyers, who were prepared to fight the charges on the grounds that the video's material about safe sex, political activism, and self-acceptance disqualified it from prosecution under the city's obscenity statute, which dictates that material can be judged obscene only if, "taken as a whole, it lacks serious literary, artistic, political, or scientific value." (What the lawyers would have done if a video in a more traditional vein—say, *Butt Boys in Space* or *I Love Foreskin*—were at issue is another question.) In any case, the charges were dropped a month later, probably due to political pressure.

The incident illustrates the hard truth that all workers in the adult-film industry have to contend with: that much of society regards their work as disreputable, if not morally bankrupt. It's one reason why the world of porn is a very insular—not to say incestuous—place. People in the industry largely socialize with other people in the industry. They live together, work together, play together, sleep together. They get tired of all the raised eyebrows, the snickers of contempt, and the leering questions they have to negotiate when they bring their work lives into more general social settings. It's easier, more comfortable to stick with their own.

By the close of 1990, Joey Stefano had reached the pinnacle of the gay video industry. It had taken just over a year. He had worked with many of the top stars and directors, had completed the film that would be the aesthetic high point of his career, and would soon take home the industry's equivalent of a best-actor Oscar. His success had even helped to rewrite the industry's rules: He'd made it to the top as a bottom, as it were, something unheard of. To put it plainly, he had nowhere to go in the porn industry but down. The only other option was to get out—and to get out meant negotiating the dangerous divide between a world where selling sex brought praise and one where it engendered prejudice. Despite the greater centrality of sex—and thus pornography—in gay culture, there remains discomfort with the kind of sexual openness that is a hallmark of the porn world. Even at the height of his success, Stefano faced a strange double standard: He was worshiped in public for his handsomeness and sexual charisma but often denigrated in private for making use of it. An item in Michael Musto's *Village Voice* column refers to the contempt Stefano was subjected to for prostituting himself—by the very people who were paying for his services. It also illustrates that even an openly gay columnist such as Musto finds it easy to resort to mockery when faced with Stefano's admittedly unusual career and its attendant sexual frankness. Musto wrote about a dinner with Stefano "before his retro-procto show-and-tell at Mars Needs Men [a gay disco]. Some cherce Stefano tidbits: 'Before I do a scene, I douche and douche and douche'; 'I'd rather get fucked by an old man than have to suck his dick'; 'There are only two stars whose assholes I'll eat'; and—drumroll, please—'I won't suck a dick if it has warts on it.' A real class act. Stefano confessed he's hired regularly by a prominent buttplug-wielding music biz honcho who, with typical hypocrisy, chides Joey for leading the distasteful life of an escort but always wants him back the next day. Joey ended the evening by sticking a beer bottle into his bad self and coining a new brand: Heinie-kin."

CHAPTER EIGHT

Doug Smith was back living in his hometown of Hollywood, Florida, when he heard from Stefano that he had moved to San Francisco. When Smith had lost his crystal connection—and only means of support—he had lived with Stefano and Karen Dior for a couple of months. Conflict with Dior soon erupted over Smith's culinary habits. He was not a big fan of peanut butter and jelly on Wonder bread, the entirety of Stefano's foodstuffs, so he consumed Dior's more sophisticated vegetarian fare, to Karen's increasing annoyance. He knew his welcome wouldn't last long. When his drugs had evaporated, so did many of his friends, and Smith had to take stock of his life. In any case he had come to see that the veneer of glamour that his drug-addled gang had kept carefully polished hid a more mundane reality: "It was a great party while I was making a lot of money dealing drugs; it was fabulous. But the party came to an end when I realized these people weren't shit, when I realized the people whose asses I was kissing the whole time were nobodies." But his friendship with Stefano had deepened, and his admiration for him had grown as Stefano's career had taken off. In fact, it had been Stefano who encouraged Smith to go back to Florida and return to school. He'd even bought Smith his plane ticket.

Stefano's drug use had continued to spiral out of control even as his career took off, and by the fall of 1990, when he parted with Karen Dior, he knew he had to break away from the environment that was keeping temptation firmly in his path. He chose San Francisco, where he didn't have a network of friends whose casual drug use might trigger his more than casual habit. He was clean for several months; despite the amount of drugs he did and the frequency with which he did them, Stefano could also turn away from them on a dime when the mood struck him. It was ultimately a dangerous ability, because he could keep returning to drugs with the idea that he could stop using whenever he wanted, even as each binge weakened his will to resist the next.

Stefano supported himself in San Francisco dancing both in the city and on the road and working for an escort service run by a man named Juan, with whom he lived and shared a close relationship. But after a few months, Stefano got the itch to return to L.A., and a fight with Juan precipitated his return. It was the spring of 1991, and Stefano was in an upbeat mood. He sat down for an interview with Sabin for the inaugural summer '91 issue of the *Gay Video Guide,* a publication founded as a resource guide for gay-porn aficionados. Unlike the skin magazines, which publish photo stills and a glowing review of a video in exchange for an ad, the *Gay Video Guide* doesn't rely on the largess of the video producers for its existence. Sabin made the decision to print it on newsprint in a small four- by six-inch format to keep costs down and maintain some independence. The quarterly magazine uses a four-star system to review dozens of videos and also includes news stories about the business, a gossip column by Gender, and a star interview in each issue.

The interview with Stefano provides a rare first-person account of his life and career. It also captures Stefano at a significant crossroads, personally and professionally. He discusses the time he spent in San Francisco as an initial attempt to get some distance on his frenzied life, to lay plans for a way to get beyond it.

STEFANO: I want to go to school for accounting and to study psychiatry.

GAY VIDEO GUIDE: I thought that was why you had moved to San Francisco.

STEFANO: I tried to get into two schools there, but I wanted to come back here. I went to San Francisco to get sober—from everything.

GAY VIDEO GUIDE: When I first interviewed you (*Thrust,* 1989), you'd just gotten back on track after falling off the wagon. You were just starting out in this business. Then success hit really big, and you fell off the deep end...

STEFANO: Yeah, I was really into drugs.

GAY VIDEO GUIDE: I think you cleaned yourself up a couple of times while you were living here...

STEFANO: Only once!

GAY VIDEO GUIDE: Okay, only once. So why was leaving L.A. the answer? Were the drugs too accessible here?

STEFANO: No. I had support up in San Francisco. I always went up to San Francisco even if I was fucked up or not. I had to get out of West Hollywood! I had to get out of the business for a while, and I thought that moving was the answer, and it was. Now I know I can live anywhere and stay sober and go to meetings—so there! That was my problem. I fell off the wagon once, so I moved out here from Philly, then I fell off again, and I moved away again. I sort of lost myself…

GAY VIDEO GUIDE: Was it the money?

STEFANO: It wasn't the money. The money was just another thing added to it. When I was using before and living in Philadelphia, I just had to struggle more to get it. But I still would get high. When I came out here and got into videos, I didn't have to worry about getting the drugs or paying the rent and stuff like that, 'cause I had the money. I got high more often. I did do more drugs. It wasn't like I got beat up; it was more emotional. I lost myself in this business. I was everywhere. I said yes to every movie that was offered to me. Doing everything for everybody. I got caught up with "Joey," and I lost who I was.

Sabin and Stefano discuss the difficult point that Stefano had reached in his video career, as he found himself suddenly less in demand by the top video producers, having to do movies for less-established companies with smaller budgets. As Stefano explains, "They'll use you until they find that next 'new' model. Falcon Video put me in three movies, and now they don't want me anymore." When Sabin points out that Stefano's current work with Gino Colbert (who was then a relatively unestablished director) is several notches below that of Falcon in the gay porn hierarchy, Stefano admits that he's simply not getting the attention—or remuneration—he used to. "Gino paid me very well," Stefano says, "and that's what concerns me now. It's like this: I was getting big money two years ago, but now I have to take less."

But if in one breath Stefano talks about finding his options curtailed in the industry, in the next he insists that he doesn't want to continue making videos. Sabin mentions the enthusiasm for the business that had animated Stefano during an interview less than two years before.

GAY VIDEO GUIDE: You told me then that you wanted to be in porno and that it was a trip to get to be with people you had fantasized about. Was it really different in reality than you expected?

STEFANO: No. It's like there's only so much you can do in porno, and then it's time to move on. I don't know how some people can last the ten or fifteen years that they've been in this business. To me, it's a waste of time and talent. Sexually, I would love to do movies all the time, but realistically and careerwise, I can't.

GAY VIDEO GUIDE: I think you've reached saturation point and that some companies think you're overexposed.

STEFANO: There are a lot more people out there who are overexposed! The fact is that I'm a name. Tony Davis has done more films than me, and yet his name isn't as well-known as mine is. For a while people didn't want to use me on box covers and all that, and that's okay.

GAY VIDEO GUIDE: Didn't that all change after you won the best actor award?

STEFANO: I've had a lot of offers, but...I just don't want to do it anymore.

GAY VIDEO GUIDE: Why?

STEFANO: I'm tired of it. It's like a trap. You see, if I keep on filming, it just goes on and on. I'm trying to get out of the money. The money's real good!

Indeed, earlier in the interview Stefano boasts of having made more than $100,000 in 1990 and $30,000 so far in 1991. When Sabin asks, "So where is it?" Stefano replies, "Um...I don't know." Not one to beat around the bush, Sabin continues to probe the issue of Stefano's future with rather startling bluntness. "And where else can you, an uneducated and untrained person, make that 'big' money?" he asks. Stefano freely admits the dilemma he faces: "That's right. I will never be able to leave it if I keep on going back to do 'just one more movie.' Twice I've tried, but I can make so much money. Even just dancing at the clubs, I do well…"

Stefano returns several times to the idea that his porn persona has become a burden that he can't escape, an alter ego that has made Nick Iacona all but invisible—and utterly meaningless—to the rest of the world. He has found that living up to the fantasies his video persona inspired is a near impossibility. "One of my regrets is that I didn't plan to be this big star," Stefano says. "Now it's 'Joey Stefano' wherever I go! It bugs me, 'cause I get a lot of attitude and hear a lot of shit for it. I can't go nowhere now. A lot of people are intimidated by me. It's hard for me to even date…. I feel that I have to stop now so I can have a life years from now. It's like I've had my feelings hurt by people because of what I do. They sometimes envy me, but then they're intimidated by me. It's like I've become this sort of a 'thing' that they want to watch but not touch. And that hurts."

When Sabin suggests that people are responding to the image—smoldering, sexy, aloof—that Stefano projects from both video screen and stage, he responds: "But I'm giving them what they want! You see, the name Joey Stefano got so big that when I would go to perform at a club, I was afraid of being a flop. They've seen me only as an image, and that was a pretty hard thing to live up to. When I would perform at a jack-off club, I'd have to give them Joey Stefano. I try so hard, and I do too much sometimes! I've done things onstage that I never do myself. I've been fisted, taken two dildos up my ass, and I would never do that in my personal life. But I'm doing this for other people 'cause it's what they expect from Joey Stefano. I feel that so much has been taken from the real me."

It's clear from the interview that Stefano was genuinely disenchanted with the industry and that some of that attitude sprang from the knowledge that his earning power in videos was rapidly dwindling. The $100,000 he had earned the year before was certainly a significant sum for a 22-year-old man, but it was not an annual salary, and the speed with which the industry embraced him was in some degree matched by the speed with which it discarded him. Although he would continue to make movies sporadically until his death, he would rarely be working for the top companies.

A variety of factors are responsible for the rapid peaking of his video career; principally, the nature of the industry itself and Stefano's lack of business acumen. In the early days of the industry, when films were actually filmed and shown in theaters, careers lasted longer. A Jack Wrangler or an Al Parker or a Kip Noll could make films for several years. Because of the expense of shooting on film, far fewer companies were producing movies, and they worked with dependable stables of talent. In addition, filmed porn movies tended to have more-developed story lines, so the performers were actually playing different characters—as with mainstream movie stars—instead of just repeating the same limited repertoire of sex acts. Audiences didn't tire of them as quickly.

The coming of the videotape era revolutionized the business, for better and for worse. It exploded the market, making the movies available to a much wider audience, not just urban or suburban audiences who had access to adult-movie theaters. For a while movies were shot on film and sold on VHS, Beta, or Super 8, but shooting on film soon was perceived as unnecessarily expensive, as upstart companies began going straight to videotape. By the late '80s, film was a thing of the past. And as videos became drastically cheaper to produce and the market for them grew, new suppliers began entering the business at a dizzying rate.

According to industry scribe Kinnick, the trend was typified and intensified by the entry into the business in 1989—just as Stefano was entering, coincidentally—of a company initially called Associated Video Group, later known as Planet Group. "Their strategy was to flood the market," says Kinnick. "Everything since 1989 in the gay video market has been a reaction against Planet Group. In the first half of the decade—1990 to 1994—half of what you saw was put out by Planet Group, but you couldn't tell this by looking at it." The company produced an arsenal of product that they marketed under a variety of different labels. Kinnick estimates that they had some 200 different names for video lines over the years. "At one point Planet Group alone was putting out three hundred movies a year under various names. The rest of the industry, combined, was putting out about that many at Planet Group's peak." (The company eventually folded, selling its catalog to HIS Video.)

The big companies had to fight the onslaught, and if Catalina and Falcon were putting out half a dozen films in the early '80s, by the '90s they were producing upwards of thirty a year. With the rocketing output came an increased need for fresh talent. If in the early '80s a star could make a dozen films over four or five or six years, by the late '80s and early '90s it would not be unusual for models to make a dozen films in less than a year. And—with rare exceptions—after a model has made a certain number of films, he is perceived as being played out; a newer name is needed and is readily found.

"It's such an incestuous industry that if it—as an industry—feels you're no longer a marketable commodity, it will no longer hire you," says Kinnick. "It's not like you find a little niche at Paramount making road pictures. In gay porn, most people peak before the industry gets tired of them; they don't want to be porn stars all their life. They work for six months, make their money, and then they leave. Many of them leave very happy."

Adds Sabin: "It used to be that models were signed by the big companies to an eight-picture deal or a six-month contract. Now it's just three movies. You do three movies for Falcon, three for Catalina, three for Forum, a few other companies—and then you're out."

The only way a performer can resist the steadily intensifying turnover rate is by strictly limiting his output and carefully steering a career plan. Indeed, the success of stars Jeff Stryker and Ryan Idol proves that despite—or perhaps because of—the deluge of product in the gay video world of the '90s, less is more. Both Idol and Stryker had handlers who know how to orchestrate a campaign around relatively few films. As "tops," they can also market ancillary products in the form of rubber approximations of their anatomical assets, marketed as the next best thing to a date with the real thing.

Stefano, pegged as a bottom, couldn't supplement his income with such sidelines and had to make more movies. "There was no product marketing with Joey. He couldn't make dildos," says Mickey Skee. "That's how Jeff Stryker makes his money, as with Rex Chandler and Ryan Idol. The three of them, combined, didn't make as many movies as Joey Stefano did."

"This is the problem with adult-film stars: How many movies do you do?" adds Jerry Douglas. "The standard advice is to do as few films as you can afford to do, and your career will last longer. There's an inevitable arc of a career; the more you do, the less people want to see you. I always tell actors to

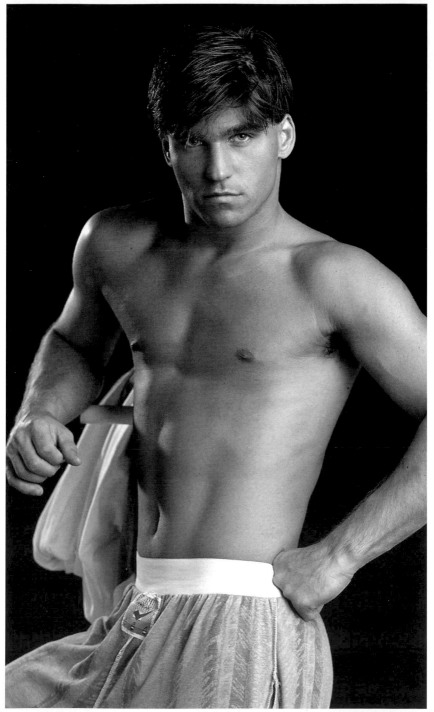

Before starting his career in gay porn, Joey Stefano had supported himself as a hustler

BILLBOARD

JOEY STEF

THE RIVER

THE LEGEND OF JOEY STEFANO

Stefano appeared in dozens of videos during his five years in the gay porn business, quickly becoming a featured player

Publicity stills from Stefano's golden age as a star

The feminine influences (clockwise from left): Karen Dior, Chi Chi LaRue, and Sharon Kane

Stefano, shortly before his death at age 26 from a drug overdose

find something new to do in every film, even if it's just something like giving someone a hickey. If you can find one thing new to do every time, it'll stretch your career." The publicity mileage Idol and Stryker have derived from the gradual expansion of their sexual repertoires, from being passive to active participants, proves the point.

Stefano entered the business as an eager, sexually adventurous kid looking to live out his fantasies. He had no master plan and didn't have the inclination to develop one. He didn't think about the long term; he was living for the moment and didn't realize that each video he did depleted the only capital he had: the appeal of his sexuality.

"Most performers burn out very quickly," says Douglas. "And everyone wanted Joey. He was a dream to work with at the beginning: sexually dependable, not a prima donna. And he went through money; he was lavish with gifts, lavish with spending. Plus he had a drug habit."

"If he had waited, his career would have perpetuated at a higher level much longer," adds Sabin. "But because he did any movie that was offered him, his rate immediately began falling."

In any case, the $100,000 Stefano made in 1990 was due primarily to income from what might be called ancillary revenues: dancing at clubs and escort work, a more rarefied name for prostitution. Despite industry players' protestations that the days of exploitation in the business are over, the performers' video contracts are inherently exploitative. For a one-time fee of $500 to $1,500 on average, a model signs over to the video producer all rights to his performance; there are no royalties granted and no additional payments, even if scenes are used in more than one movie, as they often are. And there is certainly no health plan. Although porn performers who reach star status can negotiate better contracts, Stefano, at the height of his earning power, was too scattered, too caught up in the excitement of having sex with the new model who'd caught his eye to demand the kind of money he could've had. While other performers call directors looking for work when they need money, Stefano, according to director Jim Steel, would call when he'd seen a new man he wanted to work with. The money was incidental.

Stefano's friends had urged him from the beginning to be sensible with his money. On the set of *Buddy System II,* his first video, Gino Colbert sat him down and gave him the same speech he'd been given by veteran porn star Vanessa Del Rio when Colbert was starting his porn career. "I told him that you've got to take the money you make and put it away, spend only what you have to," recalls Colbert. "You're gonna go through a lot of money in this business. It's gonna last two years, maybe three, and then you'll be an old name." (Just a year later, Colbert saw Stefano autographing copies of the *Adam Gay Video Directory* at Drake's, a well-known erotica boutique on L.A.'s Melrose Avenue, and Stefano sheepishly admitted to not following his advice—and regretting it.) Karen Dior too had attempted to get Stefano to put his money to good use. "He was making all this money, and yet he never had any," Dior says. "He'd get a pile and then spend it all on Wonder bread and Ecstasy. So I would urge him to buy a car or put a down payment on a car; he would say that he planned to, that he was going to start saving next week."

Next week never came, of course, and so, at the time of his *Gay Video Guide* interview, Stefano was again planning to leave Los Angeles—and thus the business—to move to New York and break into more mainstream forms of entertainment. "I'm studying acting," he told Sabin. "A legitimate stage producer in New York approached me last year and asked me when I was really going to put my talents to use. He got me thinking, and I've decided to study dancing by taking lessons from a choreographer, study acting and speech, 'cause that producer wants to cast me in his stage play. So I'm going to do that for six to eight months, and by the time I come back out here, I'm going to have enough money to buy a house or at least put a down payment on one."

Indeed. This is naïveté at its most sadly charming. The idea that a fledgling stage actor—even were Stefano to become one in the space of six to eight months—could make enough money to put a down payment on a refrigerator, let alone a house, is quixotic. And this was not the first "producer"—legitimate or otherwise—who had "approached" him. As soon as his porn career had gained momentum in early 1990, Stefano had met his share of players in the world of mainstream entertainment. He had been doing escort work—"seeing clients," in the euphemism for the euphemism—since his body had become a known one. Many porn stars supplement their income—in fact, earn most of it—through this more-upscale prostitution. Some use the video business primarily as a form of advertisement for their services. Lesser names advertise in magazines and gay papers; the major names work for agencies. Whether Stefano worked for an agency in Los Angeles is unclear, but he soon established a client list.

The decision to do escort work wasn't exactly an agonizing one for Stefano. He had hustled for drug money in Philadelphia from an early age. In fact, he initially took satisfaction in the knowledge that he had moved up the financial scale. "One of the things he was so proud about was that he didn't have to hustle anymore," says Doug Smith. Stefano joked to friends, "A thousand dollars a night—and more if you want me to move." Karen Dior remembers his occasional aversion to a job as a matter of mere laziness: "[One of L.A.'s biggest music moguls] used to pay him $1,000 to go have sex with him. Once, when we were all living at the Confetti and Nick didn't want to go, not because he didn't want to turn a trick but because he was lazy and didn't want to go to work, Chi Chi said, 'Girl, it's a thousand bucks—for an hour! Go do it.'"

It was on a call to the same music mogul, Smith recalls, that it was brought home to Stefano that if he had moved up the scale in his own eyes, an expensive prostitute, in the eyes of others, was hardly different from a cheap one. "He came home really hurt and upset," Smith says. "He felt like now he was a big porn star, but people still treated him the same way: 'Here's the money—do your thing and go.'"

His persistent naïveté is clearly illustrated here: He believed that the fame his video career had brought him would bring not only higher prices for his services but also an adjunct of respect. When it didn't, his fragile self-esteem received another jolt.

More pernicious than the slights from clients were the false promises some of them made to gain his favors. "Things were always just about to happen," LaRue recalls. "He just met a producer who was going to put him in a jeans ad. A week later he was going to be in a movie with Tom Cruise. It was all this 'Get in my car for a minute' stuff. He thought that everything people told him was the truth, and when I told him it wasn't, he'd say that I was being evil and that I was trying to hurt his feelings."

Jerry Douglas, who continued to see Stefano occasionally in New York after *More of a Man,* remembers that each new dinner date would reveal another plan just on the verge of fruition. "There was always a project in the works. 'I'm gonna be on a soap opera'; 'I'm gonna be on a talk show'; 'Somebody's writing a movie for me.' It's a big minefield for kids in the industry, because there are a lot of people with connections to people at the studios, in various parts of the main-stream industry. And if they're fucking them or hiring them, they say, 'I'm gonna do this for you and that for you. Now turn over.' That happened to Joey a lot. There were always things that looked good, that might happen. But once he turned over, that was that."

CHAPTER NINE

Stefano did in fact find himself dancing in New York, but the dancing he was doing didn't require any lessons and was not likely to land him a role in a chorus line. The Gaiety Theatre, on West 46th Street just off Times Square, is an odd little institution, referred to by its clientele, with tongue in cheek, as the Academy of Dance. You enter through a small doorway that is easy to miss in the shuffle of tourists heading to the theater. A plain poster lists the week's dancers, usually four of them, who do shows at 1:30, 3:30, 5:30, 7:30, and 9:30 weeknights and continuously from 6 p.m. until midnight Friday and Saturday. After climbing a steep staircase, you pay $10 for admission. The atmosphere inside is quaintly seedy. The walls are painted a cheap-looking purple. The theater itself is kept in a state of sepulchral gloom. There are perhaps seventy seats, most in desperate need of repair. All attention is focused on the small runway stage and its silver-tinsel curtains, whence emerge the performers one at a time to treat the audience to what signs describe as "very special dance interpretations." In between shows, porn videos are projected on a hand-lowered screen.

The patrons are an eclectic mix, although one wouldn't be far wrong in describing them generally as men of a certain age. The more enthusiastic choose seats in the front rows. But even these sport mostly blank expressions; whatever erotic somersaults their minds may be doing don't register on their faces. An occasional smile of mild pleasure, when a dancer is being particularly attentive, is the most violent emotion on display. Not that any excesses of enthusiasm are encouraged: A dour-looking security guard roams up and down, apparently looking for any signs of patrons taking excessive pleasure in the performance. The dancers perform two short sets to dance music of their choosing. In the first, they strip to their underwear before strutting offstage to generally tepid applause. A few minutes later they return to the stage, this time sans garments of any kind and in a state of moderate if unobtrusive tumescence. This portion of the performance elicits warmer applause.

The true locus of activity at the Gaiety used to be the back room, where patrons could consort briefly with models for $40 or $50. These assignations were arranged in a lobby off the side of the showroom called the lounge. It's a generous description, to say the least. There is more purpleness and some bench seating along one wall. In a corner is a soda machine—there is no bar. In another alcove are a pair of pinball machines of not very recent vintage. Since the AIDS crisis and the vigilance of recent city administrations have forced the closing of the back room, assignations have to be made for other premises, and even this is technically and strenuously forbidden. Signs every few feet assault the patrons with admonitions to abstain from sexual activity of any sort and contain labored descriptions of appropriate behavior. Dancers visiting with friends at the Gaiety must be treated with "respect and dignity": "No patron may engage in conversation with a performer which shall include a request for, a solicitation of or the agreement to engage in sexual conduct." Patrons who transgress will be "summarily ejected."

But business is transacted nonetheless. It has to be: The dancers make very little for their performances and aren't given airfare or hotel accommodations by the proprietors. If a dancer doesn't turn tricks, a gig at the Gaiety would be a losing proposition. Stefano had been an occasional dancer at the Gaiety since he had begun working in films (a patron remembers him sashaying through the lounge in the days prior to the crackdown on the back room, chanting, "I smell the fuzz, I smell the fuzz"). Now that he was domiciled in New York, in a studio apartment on Avenue A in the funky Alphabet City neighborhood, it became a regular stop on his tour. The legitimate producer he had referred to during his *Gay Video Guide* interview had not materialized; Stefano wouldn't complain when a promise fell through, LaRue recalls; he just wouldn't mention it anymore.

But the Gaiety was just one stop on the porn-star dance circuit, which extended across the country and included venues in virtually any city that had a gay bar willing to pay a performer to pack the house. The extent of the exposure required varied from city to city. New York, Miami, San Francisco, Chicago, and Washington, D.C., are the only cities whose municipal codes allow total nudity onstage. The rest require the modesty of a G-string. Dancers are usually paid from $500 to $750 a night to strip down to a G-string and can make, at most, a couple of hundred more in tips. Nude dancing or live sex shows—"jack off" shows—pay roughly double.

By all accounts Joey Stefano was a consummate performer when he was in top form, which is to say drug-free. When he began working in videos he had a handsomely formed but not spectacularly defined body; it had an appealing softness. He had since worked it into the more traditional vision of fleshly gay perfection, with sufficiently ample pectorals and a rippled stomach. He had several custom-designed ensembles made, consisting of strips of leather strategically placed for easy displacement. He also had rhythm, which was useful, and an ability to work a crowd, which was necessary.

Porn star Karl Thomas is a veteran of the dance circuit—he dances every weekend of the year, in fact—and had met Stefano at the Gaiety Theatre when he was starting out. They later became friendly, and Thomas recalls a show Stefano gave in Atlanta, during the Hotlanta party weekend, that was one of the best he'd ever seen. "The club was a hole in the wall, but he did an awesome number. He had a metal-mesh outfit, and he must have danced for 45 minutes. We were supposed to dance for only 20 or 25 minutes; it was constant tips." Stefano shared the bill with Thomas, Lex Baldwin, and Chip Daniels—no slouches in the sexy department. "He made more money in tips than all of us put together," Thomas recalls, some two or three hundred dollars.

His dancing wasn't the only thing he approached with the dedication of a seasoned professional, perhaps a little over-seasoned at times. In the *Gay Video Guide* interview he describes the lengths he'd go to in his more exotic shows to keep the crowds happy.

"Every jack-off club I did, from California to Florida, they haven't had as big a draw as me. Every dance club I stripped at, like in Florida—they had spent a lot of money to have a tent set up for Ryan Idol, and I drew in more people than he did! When Ryan puts on a show, he's just up there on the stage performing *at* the audience. I perform *with* the audience. I get off the stage and mingle with them. I have a good time, and I think they do too.

"I won't do the jack-off clubs no more, 'cause it took too much out of me. It really did. I did the Black Party in New York. I was working with Jon Vincent, and we were supposed to do a fuck scene. Jon was wearing a rubber, and I had to suck his dick, and he couldn't get hard. I felt like a total asshole! I was so frustrated. It was like he couldn't get hard! So I laid on back and told him to beat my ass, finger me—'Do whatever you want. We've got to do something!'"

Quel trouper! But he goes on to explain that his "show must go on" flair earned him only contempt from acquaintances once the night was over. The presumably sophisticated New York audience didn't differentiate between performer and person when it came to sex shows. If two people kiss onstage in a Broadway theater, it's acting; if they have sex onstage at a nightclub, it's perversion.

"Afterward all I heard from every queen around was how I got fisted in New York and how I was this big slut," Stefano continues. "Lots of rude comments. I mean, what was I supposed to do? You see, I'm an exhibitionist at heart. I can do crazy things in front of people. I feel like a Madonna. I can do things to really get an audience going because I have this image to hide behind. People don't know the real me."

Nick Iacona knew that it was Joey Stefano, his porn star persona, that people paid to see, and it was that persona that he gave them. But Stefano inhabited Iacona's body, and even if he believed the "real" person was hidden from sight, in truth he was as exposed as the assumed one. If Stefano was the performer, Iacona was the one who had to pay the psychological price of constantly being on view for public delectation, seducing dollars from leering patrons in city after city after city. As Karl Thomas puts it, "You have one personality who performs and another who is the real person. But it's not like you can flip a light switch and—boom!—you're off, or you're on." The attention paid Joey Stefano initially gave a boost to Nick Iacona's self-esteem, but eventually it became a drain on it: The more people fawned over Joey Stefano, the less valuable Nick Iacona seemed to become.

Life on the dance circuit was not an easy one. It meant long stretches away from home, adjusting to a new city every week, living out of a duffel bag (no suitcase necessary; leather straps don't wrinkle), wrangling with club owners over fees, killing time in unfamiliar places for days on end, and having to turn on the porn persona like clockwork. Stefano had a tendency to take the easy way out of boredom or anxiety by turning to drugs, and despite his sober stretch in San Francisco, he was quickly back to his old habits. It didn't help that the milieu he was working in, nightclubs, was a particularly hospitable one for controlled substances. Says one dancer who has worked the circuit: "Clubs will do anything for you to make you happy—get anything for you. It's a pharmacy. You can get drugs from the owners, the managers, the customers, the other performers. Every single club has their house drug dealers." Adds Karl Thomas: "You can tell a club's doing good because all the drug dealers hang out there; if there are no drug dealers, the club sucks."

As time went on and the monotony of working the dance circuit began to set in, Stefano would turn to drugs with greater frequency to shore up his will to perform. But on many occasions his indulging would jeopardize his ability to do his routine. In early 1992 Stefano was booked for a night at a Miami club called Libations—the emcee was Thomas. He hadn't seen Stefano since their first meeting more than two years before, and he almost didn't recognize the figure in the baseball cap who showed up to perform in a drug-induced torpor. Thomas nervously narrated as Stefano began his striptease. Normally he'd help whip up the crowd's enthusiasm, but he grew quiet as he watched Stefano stumble through his performance. What was worse, Stefano seemed oblivious to the fact that time was passing and that he was still fully clothed. Finally Thomas had to step in, exhorting, "Hey, the song's almost over—take off your pants!"

The next day they met for lunch and spent the afternoon in the sun. Stefano was embarrassed about his performance. "Gee, I guess I got a little too fucked up last night," he admitted. "I guess so," Thomas responded. "I was sure glad when you finally took your pants off." One of Chi Chi LaRue's most vivid memories of Stefano's career is a disastrous performance he caught at San Francisco's Nob Hill Theatre. "The theater was packed, and Joey showed up so whacked out on something, he shouldn't have gone on," LaRue recalls. "He went on anyway and literally stumbled around the stage, almost falling off. The audience didn't seem to care. They looked right past it. I turned to the friend he'd come with, who was also fucked up, and said, 'This is really pathetic. Why are you guys so fucked up?' He just slurred, 'Becu-u-uz...' I didn't know what to do. After he was done, I gave him a big hug and got in my car and left. It was one of the worst times I'd seen him."

Stefano had left behind in L.A. a group of friends who composed a strong if sometimes messy support group. He still talked to Sharon Kane often. Doug Smith was back in Florida going to community college; he too was in frequent contact with Stefano. In New York, Stefano began a friendship with a man named Vito Abbate. Cryptically identified in a

September 1995 *Out* magazine article about Stefano as "a self-described former Manhattan club promoter," Abbate was generous with his financial support. He treated Stefano and his friends well, buying dinners and clothing and tickets to events. But their relationship was a difficult one. Stefano confessed to Smith that he felt guilty accepting Abbate's generosity because he didn't believe he could ever care about Abbate in the way Abbate cared about him. Perhaps because he had been selling his sexual services since he was in his late teens, Stefano had an aversion to tainting his personal relationships with the air of commerce. Yet he hesitated to end a relationship with one of the few people in New York he could depend on for emotional—or financial—support.

In November 1991, Abbate, Sharon Kane, Stefano, and a few of Abbate's friends from New York flew to Miami for White Party weekend, an annual festival on the gay circuit. Smith was living with his parents back in Hollywood, a stone's throw from Miami, and he met them in South Beach, the newly fashionable art deco district that had been rediscovered and refurbished as a destination resort. The sleepy, dilapidated section of the city had become a home for the elderly Jewish community until enterprising entrepreneurs—largely gay— had spied in its strip of faded beachfront deco facades an opportunity to capitalize on the gay tourist dollar. And where the gay tourist dollar goes, the hipoisie soon follow, and South Beach soon became a top attraction for Manhattanites.

Stefano had been down to visit Smith once before, and Smith had had to drag him away from South Beach to meet his family. "It was like pulling teeth," he recalls. "He didn't want to leave South Beach; he wanted to be right in the middle of things, to do it all so fast and not be bothered by anything that would divert him from getting laid or finding a husband or being successful." But he charmed Doug's family, who knew that Stefano's friendship had inspired Smith's decision to return to Florida and get his life back on track. And his smashing looks easily seduced Smith's sister, who instantly formed a crush. Smith himself saw a side of Stefano on the visit that hadn't come to the fore during their West Hollywood days. "I learned that he could eat like a normal person, have a normal conversation," Smith says. "Normally he wouldn't stop to chew—he'd order this huge meal at Denny's, and it was gone in five minutes."

But the White Party weekend was one spent in the fast lane. Stefano's drug intake had reached superhuman levels, and Kane remembers the weekend as a turning point in her own ongoing battle with overindulgence. "I was up for a week with Doug and Joey," she says. "Literally up the whole time, doing drugs." They spent nights crawling the cluster of gay clubs that had sprung up and spent the days recovering from the night before. Except Stefano, for whom there seemed to be no end to the night before; Kane remembers watching in amazement as he did Special K while lying on the beach in the heat of the afternoon. As might be expected from a drug developed as an animal tranquilizer, Special K's effect is to remove the mind from its connection with the body. The heavy user enters a state called a "K hole," in which he's more or less catatonic, immobilized, incoherent. And Stefano was nothing if not a heavy user; from the beginning Smith had noticed that while others did Special K in "bumps," Joey did entire lines. He also preferred to shoot it up for a stronger and more immediate high, while most people snort it.

"He liked downers," says Kane. "He liked to just get out; in some ways he wanted to not feel, to lose control, be numb." It was a difficult state in which to go nightclubbing, and Kane remembers watching Stefano "holding up a wall" at a club that weekend, utterly immobile. Whether it was the effects of the drugs or lack of sleep or a visitation from a higher power, Kane heard the call of a voice as she lay on the beach urging her to get off the party train—"Get thee out of West Holly-wood," as she puts it. When she returned to L.A., she did just that, moving to Venice and withdrawing for a while from the frenzy of the gay-porn party scene.

Back in New York, Stefano returned to gigs at the Gaiety and dance tours interspersed with the occasional trip to L.A. for a video shoot. Although his star had dimmed in the eyes of the industry, he remained a draw at clubs, and though he no longer was in demand at the top tier of video companies, old friends like Gino Colbert gave him regular work.

In Colbert's opinion, "Chi Chi had used him up, put him on as many magazines and used him in as many movies as was humanly possible, and overexposed him." Nor did Stefano seem particularly interested in his craft, though he didn't turn down the work. "He never mouthed off on the set, but he was totally undisciplined as a performer," Colbert continues. "I was shocked. I thought at this point in his career, having done so many movies, he would be more disciplined. In the middle of a take, doing lines, he'd look right into the lens of the cam-era, like he didn't give a shit. He ruined many takes. I had to give up; I had to get as much coverage of other people so I could cut away from him when he fucked up. It's not that he didn't care, but there was a lack of love for his craft. He want-ed to do a good job, but he wasn't totally serious. It was his career at this point, and he didn't know what else to do."

His desultory performances might easily have been explained by the fact, already proclaimed repeatedly in the *Gay Video Guide* interview, that he didn't want to continue doing video work: "I get bored with not having to work a real job and having all this free time on my hands. I need new things and goals in my life. Like, movies are just not where it's at! It's been fun. It was an experience. It gives me something I could really write about. There is so much stuff that you go through with this business, so many areas that you touch—the money, the sex, the drugs, the fears—that if you don't overcome them, you're going to get lost. You know, I try to help any new porn star that comes into the business, because some people are so naive that they get eaten up. Lex Baldwin is a nice guy who I thought I'd like to work with. But to be honest with you, I don't think he's gonna make it. He's only twenty years old! He could never perform at a jack-off club or just dance in a G-string. When I come to think of it, there aren't many people who can really do this. You gotta have a good head."

In retrospect, of course, it's a hauntingly apt appraisal of the hurdles porn performers face. Clearly Stefano knew that his career path wasn't an easy one to navigate, psychologically speaking. He saw the danger of getting "lost"; but in the spring of 1991, newly sober and planning to make a gradual exit, he was confident that he had escaped the pitfalls of the business. Was it cockiness, bravado, or true confidence that made him talk so cavalierly, as one who had come out the other side and could give survival tips to beginners? He was surely right in believing that few people could expose themselves to rooms full of strangers night after night without paying a heavy spiritual price; after months spent on the road, the cracks in his confidence began to show. As 1991 turned to 1992 and an endless series of dance gigs stretched before him, it was becoming clear that Nick Iacona was not one of the sturdy few. But he could no longer support himself on video work even had he preferred to return to it exclusively. He had to dance—and trick—to stay afloat, until he found a way to get out of the business. But Stefano had always been unable to make long-term plans and stick to them. Far easier than getting out of the business was getting out of his head—temporarily and repeatedly—through Special K or other drugs. As long as he allowed himself the option of escaping the pain or tedium of his life by getting high, he wouldn't have the will to take the hard steps necessary to change it.

CHAPTER TEN

It wasn't just dissatisfaction with his career that fueled the anomie plaguing the last years of Stefano's life. He had also learned in late 1990 that he was HIV-positive. He told Doug Smith over the phone, in a halting voice, choking out the traditionally foreboding phrase: "I have something to tell you…" He was clearly upset but decided he didn't want to tell Smith after all. But Smith had guessed what it was; he couldn't think of anything else that Stefano would be so upset about. It was not a surprise to Smith and couldn't have been one to Stefano either. "He never had safe sex," Smith says flatly. "And he was always sharing needles too." Stefano began taking medication sporadically and over the next couple of years would gradually open up to his friends about it. But he knew that in his line of work it was an explosive issue, and as long as he needed to rely on work in the porn industry to support himself, it would need to be kept a secret. Because he was a "bottom," the risk to his sexual partners—who used condoms—was minimal.

But even the whisper of a rumor about an actor's HIV status is a hot-button topic in an industry that has traveled a rough road toward coming to terms with the AIDS epidemic. For obvious reasons, the issue is a central one in gay porn. In the early '80s, the first years of the epidemic, the workings of the disease and its mode of transmission remained shrouded in mystery. The porn industry was not alone in citing the lack of hard facts about the disease as reason enough to continue operating as before. In 1983, when Michael Callen and Richard Berkowitz published a booklet called *How to Have Safe Sex in an Epidemic: One Approach,* they were criticized by Gay Men's Health Crisis, one of the organizations in the forefront of activism about the disease, for the suggestion that gay men should begin "avoiding the exchange of potentially infectious bodily fluids." As evidence began to mount supporting the idea that HIV was most likely contracted during anal sex, gay health organizations began endorsing the use of condoms and spermicidal lubricants as protection. But the gay-porn industry continued to ignore the guidelines well into the mid '80s and beyond. Their rationale is understandable: The idea of introducing a condom—and thus the fact of AIDS and the specter of death—into a sex scene seemed aesthetically foolhardy. The function of pornography is to titillate, not terrorize; the idea of death is not commonly held to be an aphrodisiac. And because the industry operated on the fringe of legality, well outside the observation of the mainstream activist community, they could continue to ignore the obvious: that unprotected anal sex could be fatal. Indeed, though there is, of course, no knowing whether they contracted the virus during sex for work or sex for play—and many didn't enter the business until condom use became mandatory—almost 50 gay porn stars have succumbed to the disease.

"It took people a long time—much too long—to include rubbers," says Jerry Douglas. "They aesthetically were considered unattractive. It's the old joke: Fucking with a rubber is like taking a shower with a raincoat on. In a way it's true. I will give the industry credit: In the early days of the epidemic, when no one knew much about the virus or how it was transmitted, as soon as nonoxynol-9 came on the market, everyone started using it. Chuck Holmes said, 'We just take those turkey basters and fill them full of nonoxynol-9.' At that time that was a decent attempt."

Dave Kinnick sees 1987 as the year in which the industry finally began to acknowledge that a video camera was not a prophylactic against sexually transmitted diseases: "In terms of the way movies were made, things didn't change until '87; then there were condoms on the set, and there was often a small informational moment before filming during which it was made clear that condoms were available. But for another two years it wasn't mandatory.

"Around '88, '89, there was pressure within the industry to self-police. One of the problems had been that there weren't many rules in the industry—except ways to avoid prosecution. There had been no rules about what's done and not done, what's right and not right. But by around '89, almost everyone was using rubbers in every scene."

The one notable exception was Falcon Video, which lagged behind the other companies in taking to rubbers, probably because as the premier producer, they could get away with it.

Nick Iacona entered the business in 1989, and in his interview with *Thrust* magazine, after he'd made about ten films, he says he tested negative shortly before moving to L.A.:

"Before I came out here I had an AIDS test, and I'm clean, and in my personal life I use rubbers, so I don't do anything unsafe." Though his friends attest that the latter half of that statement isn't remotely true, there's no reason to believe he wasn't being honest about his HIV status.

By the time he began working in videos, use of condoms was the norm but, as his videos attest, by no means universal. Without exception, condoms are used in the anal sex scenes in Chi Chi LaRue's videos with Stefano. But in Catalina's *Hard Steal,* Rod Phillips does not wear a condom in his scene with Stefano; instead, we see him insert a sort of plastic syringe up Stefano's backside—a syringe filled with what is presumably a spermicidal lubricant—before they go to it. (Phillips went on to die of a drug overdose after a battle with AIDS in June 1993, but he and Stefano had a relationship both prior to and during the filming of *Hard Steal,* and it's likely that they practiced even less-safe sex offscreen.) Karen Dior distinctly recalls Stefano's agonizing over whether or not to do a Falcon video in 1990 for which it had been made clear that a condom would not be used. He had addressed that issue in the *Thrust* interview as well: "In the movies, they should be used," he says in answer to a question about safety in the business. "You have to think about the other model. You have to. That's like killing yourself. I had the chance to do two movies for Falcon, but without rubbers. I chose not to do them. I talked to them [to see] if there was any way they could use me with a rubber. If they want you bad enough, they'll use a rubber on you." As a bottom, he knew it was dangerous, but whether he changed his mind because of Falcon's preeminence in the business or for other reasons, Stefano went ahead and shot a Falcon video without using a rubber, and he later regretted it. "It was a big concern," says Dior. "He wished afterward that he hadn't done it." The movie was *Plunge,* and his scene was with Lon Flexx, who would die of AIDS complications in 1995.

But Stefano's concern about being put at risk in his video for Falcon is in odd contrast to the less-than-vigilant attitude he took toward safe sex in his private life. It almost seemed he thought sex for work was somehow more dangerous than extracurricular activities. In addition to the Falcon Video incident, Dior recalls an occasion when one of Stefano's most prominent escort clients offered to triple his fee—from $1,000 to $3,000—if Stefano would let him forgo a condom. It upset Stefano, and he declined. When he was sober and was forced to face the issue, he acted sensibly—or tried to. But his appetite for sex was voracious and constant, and he would binge on sex as he binged on drugs—often when he binged on drugs. "He was pretty promiscuous," recalls Kane, with whom Stefano crashed when he came to L.A. "When he stayed with me, he got very sexually compulsive; he would cruise the parking lot behind Circus of Books—not for money, just to do it. He was fairly openly sexually compulsive; he admitted it, and at one point he even did therapy for it." Amusingly, the cynosure of the gay-porn world would flip through escort ads in L.A.'s gay papers and make appointments with other models. He would pay fellow porn star Jake Tanner and others for sexual encounters, creating on his own dime the kind of teaming producers regularly paid for.

And much of the sex he was having was unsafe. "This was back when we knew about AIDS and we knew we should be using condoms, but people didn't," admits Dior. Indeed, it's easy to ascribe Stefano's penchant for unsafe sex as a form of self-destruction—and there is probably an element of truth to the idea. But his behavior was by no means aberrant among urban gay men of his age. It may have been unusual in its volume, but it was not extraordinary in kind. Even with the knowledge that AIDS had claimed tens of thousands of lives, young gay men of all social strata continued to have unsafe sex—occasionally or inveterately—into the '90s. Although AIDS education made rapid strides in decreasing the infection rate among the gay population in general, unsafe sex among young gay men remained a potent problem—and still does.

The problem is not a lack of education—the problem is youth. The aberration was not Stefano's heedlessness; a disbelief in the reality of death is common to youth—that's why they make the best soldiers. The aberration was the disease. Young people of previous generations could sow their wild oats, and a gradual receding of high spirits would be followed by the onset of middle age. For gay men of Stefano's generation, the sowing of wild oats was often a fatal enterprise.

Further reinforcing the '90s nihilism of which Stefano's life, with its aimlessness and drug dependency, is a prime example was the economic recession that swept the country in the wake of Reaganomics. As the postwar boom ground resoundingly to a halt, the limitless opportunities that greeted baby boomers were replaced by much more circumscribed expectations. Pundits began declaring again the death of the American dream as upward mobility was replaced by desperate entrenchment and the occasional downward slide. The post–baby boomers faced adulthood with a diminished view of life's possibilities that was forever being contrasted with the unlimited boons previous generations had reaped. The message was clear, and for gay men it coincided all too aptly with the realities of AIDS: The future was simply not what it was cracked up to be. Perhaps the most natural reaction was the road Stefano had taken—to live for today.

His AIDS diagnosis came as a sad affirmation of what Stefano had seemed to feel in his bones since his father's death had shaken all of life's certainties: The future could not be depended on to keep its promises. It was the same message his generation was hearing on the nightly news. Stefano's reaction was to believe in making the most of the moment, not postponing one's pleasures, only to see one's chance at them evaporate with time. Also contributing to his belief that the promises of tomorrow were hollow ones was the fact that the many offers of more legitimate performance work that had been offered by clients—the soap opera, the theater gig, the movie—had invariably fallen through.

But life went on despite the uncertainties, despite Stefano's sometimes fatalistic attitude. (In a rare introspective talk with Mickey Skee one day, Stefano said he was afraid of turning thirty, that he thought thirty was old, that he didn't want to see his body deteriorate. "I don't see myself living past thirty anyway," he concluded.) He came to terms with his HIV status on a personal level, picking up a book about living with HIV that he kept with him when he traveled and telling close friends he could handle it. Kane recalls that "it upset him because he always wanted to have kids; that was the main thing that bothered him." But regarding his personal well-being, "I think he kind of said, 'Fuck it!'" Kane continues. "'Who knows when I'm gonna die, so I'm just gonna go out with a bang.'"

Professionally, however, HIV was still an inflammatory issue. Although all video companies had begun vigilantly using condoms by the time Stefano was diagnosed, the mystery of HIV contagion made the issue a troublesome one nevertheless. "If an actor is known to be HIV-positive, he'll never work again," says Mickey Skee flatly. Sabin concurs, almost verbatim: "If an actor is known to be HIV-positive, companies won't hire him." But the issue seems to be not whether an actor is in fact HIV-positive but whether it is a matter of public knowledge. "Most directors I know will publicly say they would never use anyone who's HIV-positive—and yet they all have," says Skee. "It's a small business, and rumors travel very fast."

Stefano's HIV status would remain a sort of open secret in the industry. "He was one of the first names in the business to tell people he was HIV-positive," says Skee, "but then he denied it, because he knew that although he was in New York not making movies, that reputation would really destroy him." Stefano was also among the first porn stars to regularly volunteer for AIDS fund-raisers, though some organizations turned up their noses.

Typical of that reaction to the adult-film industry's attempts to aid the AIDS fund-raising effort was the response Sabin and Mickey Skee received when they planned the first *Gay Video Guide*–sponsored Gay Erotic Video Awards. The awards were conceived both as an alternative to the AVN Awards—where some felt the gay videos were given short shrift—and as an AIDS fund-raiser. But the event's creators had trouble finding an organization that would take their money. "We went to every major AIDS fund-raiser in the country, and the only one that would take us was Aid for AIDS," recalls Skee. "They all said that our industry promotes unsafe sex." By 1992 that was untrue, and, indeed, Sabin and Skee, writing for the *Gay Video Guide* and *Adult Video News,* respectively, had a hand in forcing the few video companies that lagged behind the others in using condoms to clean up their acts. In their video reviews they would pointedly mention any failure to take the proper precautions.

That Stefano remained one of the gay porn industry's most fabulous creations, though he was no longer one of its most highly paid workhorses, was obvious from the prominent role he played in that first awards show, held in November 1992 at Los Angeles's Arena nightclub. Chi Chi LaRue hosted the somewhat slapdash proceedings with ribald flair. Hordes of porn-star newcomers and veterans trooped on and off the stage, leaving in their wake the papers on which their scripted speeches were written, so that by the end of the evening the black stage was littered in white scraps of paper. The microphones worked intermittently.

Stefano presented an award with Warhol veteran Holly Woodlawn and was nominated himself in the Best Supporting Actor category for his role in *Prince Charming,* a Jim Steel video enlivened by some amusing pseudomedieval camp trappings. He played the stable boy who puts the prince in his place. Just before he beds the prince, however, he rips off the regent's crown and tosses it away; it clatters like a Coke can. (Even the box-cover text wittily sent up the royal melodrama genre: "Who will be king? Who will fall victim to mean, dominant stable boy Joey Stefano? Who will face evil Chinese soothsayer Moo Goo Shang Hai? Who thinks of this stuff? Queens.") But Stefano lost the award.

He was also scheduled to dance with fellow star Matt Gunther, but the boys had a tiff backstage, Mickey Skee remembers. "They were about to go onstage together, and they got in a fistfight. I grabbed Nick, Sharon grabbed Matt, but Nick still got a bloody nose. I think Matt Gunther was concerned about how much stage time they would each get. Nick wanted to go home but ended up going on to do a towel dance by himself." (There was indeed no love lost between Stefano and Gunther. In a 1991 interview with Dave Kinnick, who had complimented him on his taste, Gunther said—after ensuring that the tape recorder was running—"Compare my taste to someone like Joey Stefano, who has no taste—who shops probably at one of those tacky little shops off La Brea where you get your sofa and love seat together for $325, and it's made of fake leather, and you think it's perfectly lovely.")

For Skee the dance proved as unnerving as the brawl—Skee was in charge of making sure the show proceeded without a hitch. Under rules laid down by the state Alcoholic Beverage Control Department, the show was allowed to have either nudity or alcohol, not both. Serving soda to a couple of hundred of porn's proudest at a nightclub was not an option, so the nudity was nixed, and Skee and Sabin spent the evening carefully monitoring flesh exposure. "Nick did his dance with a very amazingly draped towel. He'd let it fall, and his boner would hold it up," remembers Skee, who sat backstage praying that the force of gravity would not prove greater than Stefano's enthusiasm. Happily it didn't.

Stefano was competing in another category that evening as well—Biggest Bitch on the Set—against fellow nominees Jeff Stryker, Chi Chi LaRue, and Matt Gunther, his combatant from earlier in the evening. Gunther took home the prize, apparently to no one's surprise. The award was decorously dropped from subsequent awards shows.

Although he went home empty-handed and although Ryan Idol—whose first movie Stefano had appeared in—was the most lionized star of the evening, being chosen to unveil the Video of the Year award, Stefano nonetheless had a feather in his cap more envied than any statuette. As LaRue had reminded the crowd when introducing his dance routine, Stefano had claim to a kind of fame that put all others in the shadow: He had been touched by the grace of the muse of gay men the world over, Saint Madonna herself.

Searching to explore the less-celebrated varieties of modern sexual expression for her book *Sex,* Madonna and entourage had descended on the Gaiety Theatre and, seeing the glamour in its seediness and the undeniable beauty of the dancers, chose it as the setting for the book's generous ten-page nod to gay male sexuality. (However, given the percentage of the book's buyers who were gay men, she might have been a little more magnanimous.) Stefano was among the dancers handpicked by Madonna to cavort with her, Daniel de la Falaise, and Udo Kier on and around the Gaiety stage while Steven Meisel trained his cameras on the proceedings. Indeed, images of Stefano are spread liberally across the pages, his trademark screaming-skull tattoo and long hair easily distinguishing him from the other boys. In the most arresting photograph, he lies on the floor backstage, leaning against a doorway. Next to him are two mirrors, in which we see reflected a besequined Madonna embracing a man in evening dress. Only Stefano is looking into the camera; he peers with a single eye around a curtain of hair, his lips caught between a smile and a pout. It's a breathtakingly sexy look; he seduces the camera through the smallest corner of an eye. In it Stefano is the perfect embodiment of the kind of edgy masculine beauty, tattoos and all, that was the staple of many an ad campaign in the '80s and '90s. We get a hint of his untapped potential, what might have been if he had been more enamored of the respectable mode of achievement available to the beautiful—fashion modeling—and not enraptured by pornography. Men of his beauty are far rarer in adult films than they are in fashion pages, for that reason; most, if given the option, would choose to pursue a career in fashion modeling rather than pornography. But it wasn't until the porn-starstruck Stefano had entered the business and began garnering the kind of attention he did that he realized the power of his looks. "He never thought he was gorgeous," recalls LaRue, and perhaps there is no more powerful expression of his low self-esteem.

Stefano had been thrilled to be in the Madonna book and talked excitedly of it to friends. Here at last was a "legitimate" gig of a sort, involving perhaps the biggest pop star in the field. But the pay was "legitimate" too: Stefano complained that he was paid only $150 for the shoot. And in truth, though it was published by Warner Books, an arm of one of the giants of the mainstream entertainment business, and involved the queen of the pop pantheon, for Stefano the work was scarcely different from his usual gigs. He was still naked and still onstage at the Gaiety Theatre. That Madonna was preening in sequins beside him didn't change the fact.

And though it is to her credit that Madonna saw the Gaiety as a worthy vehicle for her remarkable mythmaking abilities, the photos are indeed mythical, more illusion than reality. When Madonna and Co. packed up and left the Gaiety, they took the tawdry chic that reeks from the pages of *Sex* with them. They left behind the mundane reality and the boys who had to live with it seven days a week. When the book was released, the pages shot at the Gaiety were mounted and hung on the wall of the lounge, pointing up rather baldly the contrast between the world Madonna and her magic-makers had created and the theater's true atmosphere.

Sharing a few photo frames with Madonna did not prove to be an entrée for Stefano into more-mainstream showbiz pursuits, although it may have inspired him to put together a legitimate modeling portfolio, a plan that he pursued haphazardly until his death. By this point in his career, he probably didn't expect great things to come of a sprinkle of stardust from Madonna's wand. His naive belief in the big break around the corner had soured into an acknowledgment that things could be taken only for what they were, not as indicators of what might be coming. A $150 shoot was just that. Only after his death would Stefano's name again be linked with Madonna's, as an enterprising British tabloid, the *Sunday Mirror,* attempted to capitalize on their fleeting connection by propounding the theory that they had slept together. MADONNA'S BOYFRIEND IN AIDS SUICIDE RIDDLE, the December 4, 1994, headline screeched. DEATHBED CONFESSION OF GAY FILM HUNK WHO POSED NAKED WITH POP QUEEN. The story's fanciful reimagining of their relationship bears only a glancing resemblance to reality: Stefano, a "former boyfriend" of Madonna's, treated to "wild parties at her mansion," tells a friend on his deathbed that Madonna "had turned her back on him because he had become a junkie" and that he never told Madonna "about the result of his medical tests." That at least is certainly true. His acquaintance with the star had hardly been conducive to the sharing of intimacies; like Stefano's celebrity escort clients, Madonna had contracted with him for certain specific services. When those were duly rendered, he and the pop star parted ways, she to return to the comforts and trials of her life in the world's spotlight, he to a life whose increasing difficulty had only been thrown into relief by the momentary illumination of it by her court photographer's flashbulb.

CHAPTER ELEVEN

By 1993, Stefano's reputation in the video industry had soured considerably. He had always had prima donna potential; in the beginning it was part of his charm and was considered perfectly acceptable behavior from a reigning beauty. But what was tolerated from a star at the peak of his popularity wasn't likely to be put up with from a performer in decline, and Stefano, rather than recognizing the limits of his appeal and taming his behavior, got progressively worse. He wasn't happy in his work, and the nature of the work made it very easy for him to spread his malaise.

Karen Dior was getting ready to direct a bisexual video titled *Bi-Golly* when he got a call from Sharon Kane imploring him to put Stefano in a movie. Stefano had been staying with Kane regularly when he came to L.A. and had borrowed money from her that she needed. By this time Stefano's video fee had dropped from a high of more than $1,500 per scene to a mere $500 or $600—scale, basically, for gay porn movies. Dior was reluctant to cast him; he had been on enough sets with Stefano in recent years to know that he was not easy to work with and had vowed not to put him in one of his own productions. But he cast Stefano nonetheless, wanting to help Kane, whose predicament he could sympathize with in light of the financial roller coaster he'd shared with Stefano when they lived together.

Choosing an actor to pair with Stefano had by this time become a delicate and dangerous art. "He was always picky about the people he worked with," recalls LaRue, who last worked with Stefano on 1992's *Songs in the Key of Sex.* "I could usually pick people that he wanted to work with, but eventually you would put him with just about anybody, and it wouldn't work." For his scene in *Bi-Golly,* Dior chose a shy, easygoing actor, Tad Bronson, who was eager to work with Stefano. Dior knew better than to choose a novice—always a recipe for disaster—and made sure that Stefano's costar had learned the ropes. It didn't help.

The day of the shoot began badly. Bronson had politely arrived early, and when Stefano showed up late, he made it fairly clear that his costar was not to his liking. "I can't believe I have to work with him," he said baldly, not troubling to hide his disdain from his costar. Bronson was understandably mortified but remained good-natured. Dior gave Stefano the option of forgoing the shoot, but he declined, and they got to work, though a distinct pall had already begun to gather over the set.

Although he had agreed to move his body in front of the video cameras, Stefano did little else to facilitate the process as the day progressed. With the videotape rolling, the lights in place on the kitsch Western set, and his scorned costar valiantly fellating him, Stefano broadcast his boredom to all corners of the room, sighing heavily and rolling his eyes as Bronson attempted to get a sexual response out of him against his will. "The guy is sucking his dick, and Nick's got a bored expression on his face. He'd say, 'You're not doing it very good!'" remembers Dior, whose dismay can well be imagined. "I told the cameraman not to shoot his face or to try to sneak a shot of his face when he was looking halfway happy. We tried to work around it." Things got only worse when a little more cooperation from Stefano was required. The anal sex portion of the day's entertainment proved particularly disastrous.

"The guy was trying to fuck him, and Nick was not cooperating," says Dior. "You can work with a person, or you can fight it. If you don't want a dick in your butt, you can position yourself to make it very difficult." Stefano readily found that position and remained there. To add insult to injury, he blamed the difficulty on his hapless costar, complaining, "It's not hard enough! It's not my fault. Get it hard!" Small wonder that his partner had indeed begun to lose enthusiasm for the task at hand, jeopardizing the outcome of the scene, which, by the unwritten law of porn video, needed to end as all others do: with ejaculation—the come shot, the money shot.

In desperation, Dior took Stefano aside and gave him an ultimatum: "I told him he wasn't being helpful and that if we didn't get the scene, he wouldn't be paid. There had to be some sort of happy conclusion to this scene." Because of the unpredictable nature of the business, there are always a few alternatives a director can turn to if a scene isn't working. "I gave him some options," Dior says. "Someone on the set could be a stunt dick; I had already approached people about it and found two or three people who had agreed to do it. So we could get a few closeups of him getting fucked and fake the rest. Or we could use a dildo." In high dudgeon at the idea of a stunt dick, Stefano opted for the inanimate alternative but was predictably stingy with the requisite groans of pleasure; his might better be described as groans of tolerance. By this time all hope of getting a money shot out of Bronson was lost, and in the end Dior had to supply the crowning moment himself, inserting it into the scene after the fact.

Stefano's attitude toward dancing was scarcely more enthusiastic, although he continued to seek out gigs because they remained a necessary source of income. He got in touch with manager Peter Scott in late 1992, and Scott agreed to book him on a three-city Texas tour in January 1993, although he was wary of Stefano's drug reputation. To ensure that Stefano remained sober—or at least functional—on the swing through San Antonio, Dallas, and Houston, Scott made arrangements to travel with him, something he didn't regularly do. But Stefano had a way of confounding the worst expectations and remained drug-free for the entire trip. He didn't exude enthusiasm for his work, however, and couldn't muster the energy for even the basic cordialities. "He came off the plane with a pair of headsets on, and it was all he could do to take them off," says Scott, who wasn't taking any chances and met his flight in San Antonio. Stefano never let down his wall of reserve. "I was with him the whole time," Scott says, "and he absolutely did no drugs or alcohol; he was totally professional. But he was aloof, even in the dressing room with the other dancers. He'd come in, put on his outfit by himself, do his exercises, and do his show. To the audience, it would have seemed like he was having a good time, but it seemed pretty robotic." Although he spent part of his time offstage turning tricks, he spent most of it talking on the phone and watching TV. "If you tried to shoot the breeze, he wasn't interested, and he'd let you know he wasn't interested," Scott continues. "He was the type of guy that you could walk in with a cast on your arm and he wouldn't say, 'What happened to your arm?' This guy was totally involved in himself—not conceited but just totally involved in himself." The years of exposing his sexual identity to the paying public—in clubs or escort work—had taken a toll. Sex can trigger emotional responses whether we intend it to or not, and Stefano's emotional closing-off, his studied aloofness, was probably a defense against letting his feelings flow too freely into his work.

It was a distancing that could also be supplied by drugs.

He did let his guard down under the right circumstances: when he was away from the pressures of New York or Los Angeles, where "Joey Stefano" had long since eclipsed Nick Iacona. One such safe haven was the home of director Robert Prion in the unassuming burg of Woodbridge, New Jersey. Prion had entered the adult-film industry through the back door. An early videotape enthusiast (the first thing he taped, on a machine purchased in 1972, he recalls, was the Emmy-winning television special *Singer Presents Liza With a Z*), he had been coaxed into taping two friends' anniversary tryst for posterity. When the tape was shown at a party, other requests followed, and Prion soon found himself with enough footage for a film. He dubbed it *The Boys of New Jersey* and showed it privately until friends urged him to seek a professional release. He continued to make the occasional movie through the '80s even as he continued his day job, working at a super-market deli. (He sometimes performed in his videos, occa-sioning some rather startled looks from across the deli counter.) The hobby became a full-time gig in 1991, when his grandmother, whom he had been taking care of, died. He kissed good-bye the twenty-two years at the deli and made porn his primary source of income. He operates well outside the gay-porn epicenter in L.A., casting his own roster of talent in his low-budget productions, which are shot in and around the cozy Woodbridge home his grandmother left him.

He had been struck by Stefano's looks in one of his early Falcon releases, and when a model he'd cast in a previous film—who goes by the name of Storm—called from San Francisco a couple of years later, where he was dancing with Stefano at the Campus Theater, they arranged for Stefano to shoot a scene in Prion's 1991 video *Total Impact*. In the video, Stefano, wearing a T-shirt with his own picture printed on it, joins a three-way already in progress; you can tell who the major name is by the contrast in hairstyles. Stefano's three partners all sport the same parted-in-the-middle, longer-in-back 'do—call it the Jersey shag—that would raise eyebrows on Santa Monica Boulevard. The scene was shot by Prion himself—he does all his camerawork—in a bedroom under the surreal, sardonic eye of a cutout of Bette Davis, circa *All About Eve*. By no means a polished, Catalina-style product, Prion's video is crude but has its own engaging intimacy. He created a casual environment that made Stefano as comfortable as possible, given that he couldn't be surrounded by the apparatus of the big Los Angeles production companies—or plenty of willing drug suppliers.

They kept in touch by phone, and Prion made plans to shoot a new video with Stefano in January 1992, though he had been worried by reports that Stefano had been jeopardizing dancing gigs with his drug use. "I was expecting doom," says Prion, who was happily surprised when Stefano showed up in fine condition. A snowstorm hit while they were shooting, and Prion offered Stefano a spare bedroom for the weekend. Although he hesitated to bring it up, having learned that Stefano could be sensitive about what he would and would not talk about, Prion asked him about the stories of dissolution he'd heard, which were in such marked contrast to Stefano's behavior at Prion's home. "He said, 'I don't know... When I'm around you I don't really need that stuff. You make me feel comfortable. You don't invite people over to show me off,'" says Prion. "He didn't like that. If he was doing a show and people were paying to see Joey Stefano, that was fine, but once he finished he didn't want to have to be that person. He said he didn't like it so much that he would do drugs to take his mind off things. He didn't like being Joey Stefano twenty-four hours a day."

When the storm cleared, Stefano was off again, and Prion, like most of Stefano's other friends and associates, would hear from him when Stefano felt the need to get in touch; he was often between phone numbers and answering services, on the road, or staying with friends. In June, Prion got a sudden, urgent call from Stefano, who in a strangled voice asked if he could come down from New York and spend the weekend: "I've got to get out of this fucking town" was the gist of it. Prion, who had just finished editing a video and was planning to be out of town himself, canceled his plans; there was a troubling note of desperation in Stefano's voice.

Stefano, Prion, and Prion's lover, Jay Richards, spent the weekend barbecuing steaks, lying by the pool, and watching Bette Davis movies on video, and Stefano, who had maintained a certain reserve during previous meetings, opened up. "I can go to the Bahamas or Acapulco with a client anytime I want," he said, "but when I come to your house, we can just sit down and watch a movie, and I don't have to worry about anybody shoving cocaine up my nose." Prion was building a small pool house, and Stefano expressed a desire to live there when it was finished. The problem, as he freely admitted, was his inability to resist temptation; like a kid who doesn't understand why he can't eat candy all the time, he didn't have the willpower to abstain from drugs when they were handy and he was in the mood. And his occupations ensured that they were always handy: "I hate going to L.A.," he told Prion. "Whenever I'm there, all I do is get fucked up." Clearly, New York was becoming equally dangerous ground. In truth, the temptations came his way not because he was in the wrong places but because he was Joey Stefano, and that was something he couldn't even escape in homely Woodbridge, New Jersey, as Prion discovered that weekend when he and Stefano popped in to the local Shop-Rite to pick up barbecue supplies. "Don't ask me why—it was bizarre—but it was like the gay parade had gone through the Woodbridge Shop-Rite. Half the customers were gay couples. Can you imagine the look on these people's faces, seeing Joey Stefano at the Woodbridge Shop-Rite? He was in a fun mood, so we tooled down the aisles with the shopping cart, watching the same couples going by us seven and eight times. He'd murmur, 'Here they come again...'; he played it to the hilt. He liked being Joey Stefano that day. He signed a couple of autographs at the checkout counter. But the people you'd meet in a New Jersey Shop-Rite aren't the ones you'd be bothered by in New York."

But back to New York he went when Monday came, only to give Prion another desperate call come September. Stefano had been in a fight with a client during a trip to the Caribbean and had arrived back in New York without any money. He had called an agent who had been lining up dance gigs for him and receiving the payment directly. But when he asked him for the several thousand dollars he knew he was owed, the agent denied it: "What money? You spent all your money." He was in tears as he told the story to Prion. "Robert, I always get taken advantage of!" he wailed. Prion took the train to the city the next day and loaned him $1,000. Despite continually expressing frustration at the way money seemed to slip through his fingers, even as earning it began to get harder and harder, Stefano couldn't seem to maintain any semblance of financial organization. If he had enough money to get where he needed to go, he was happy; if he ran out, he could turn a trick and make some more. It was a cycle that kept him from breaking the habit of a business that was becoming increasingly burdensome to his psyche and spirit.

The evidence of the strain Stefano was under—and the lengths he'd go to to diffuse it—became obvious to Prion on the third and final occasion they worked together. Stefano had attended Prion's annual Christmas party in December 1992, and Prion had been relieved to see him sober and relaxed, happy to sign boxes and posters for some of Prion's guests. He had received a dire report just weeks earlier from a bar in Albany, New York, of Stefano's dissipation. Booked to strip with another dancer, Stefano had arrived at the club clearly intoxicated and proceeded to fall off his platform. Worse still, he started performing oral sex on his dancing partner in full view of the audience, something Albany laws by no means condoned. The bar's owner and manager had to haul him off-stage, relating later that Stefano was so high, he didn't seem to know where he was.

But at the party Stefano was functional and friendly, and Prion made tentative arrangements to work together, firming up the plans over the next few months. The shoot was set for Memorial Day weekend of '93, and Prion had booked Karl Thomas and a newer model named Giovanni to work with Stefano. Thomas, who didn't do drugs and didn't like the difficulties they could cause on sets, had been hesitant despite his friendship with Stefano. He had heard the horror stories too. Prion assured him that he'd never had a problem with Stefano on his videos, but—confounding Prion's high hopes this time—Stefano climbed off the train from New York in a state that made a shoot impossible. Through his chemical torpor

Stefano was sadly contrite: "Oh, Robert, I'm so sorry, I'm so fucking sorry. I don't want to be like this around you. Oh, man, I went to this party last night, and everybody was giving me this shit, man. I didn't even know what it was, and I was taking it... I'm so sorry." Prion canceled the day's shoot and stashed Stefano in the pool house, telling Karl Thomas, who was still in the city, that Stefano was fatigued from a road trip. Stefano slept for the next eighteen hours, with Prion checking in on him a couple of times to make sure he was still breathing. When he emerged the next day, he apologized again over coffee. "He said the last thing he knew, he was at some kind of Black Party or White Party and had bumped into some friends who always gave him drugs," Prion remembers. "It was the first time he had admitted he did heavy drugs when he was in New York. You could see he was deteriorating. Before it had been an L.A. thing; now it was an everyday thing."

One cup of coffee, and Stefano was fully recovered and eager to do the shoot. He befriended Giovanni, who was a fan of Stefano's and wanted to spend some time with him before the filming, which was taking place at Giovanni's nearby condominium. Thomas arrived, and the three-way scene went off without a hitch; Thomas remembers it as being one of the most pleasurable shoots he's been on: "We laughed so much; it was hard doing a come shot when you were laughing so hard." The shoot broke up at 7 o'clock, and Stefano and Thomas got on a train back to New York City, separating at Penn Station a little after 8.

At 1 a.m. that night, Prion's phone rang. It was Stefano, "and he's out of his fucking mind," says Prion. "He's lying in a gutter with a cell phone outside some bar: 'I'm so fucked up; I don't know what I'm gonna do.' He starts crying." Stefano had managed to call Giovanni as well, and Giovanni drove into the city to get him, finding him as promised lying in the street, by himself, steps away from the entrance to a bar, now talking to another party on the cellular phone. Giovanni got him to a hospital, where his stomach was pumped. The doctors confirmed that he had been overdosing and warned that another fifteen minutes might have been enough to finish him off.

Giovanni took Stefano back to his New Jersey apartment to help him get back on his feet. After a week, during which they began a relationship, Stefano had to go back to New York for a gig. The very next night Stefano was on the phone with Giovanni again, high again, wanting to be rescued again. But once was enough for Giovanni, who was dismayed that after being drug-free for a week after an overdose, Stefano would get high again virtually the minute he stepped foot in the city. When Prion talked to Stefano a couple of days later, Stefano blamed his friends: "I hooked up with my fucked-up friends. When am I going to learn not to call them when I'm in town. But I did it again. I have no willpower." Prion didn't know what to say, thinking to himself, *Doesn't this attractive guy have any supervision?*

The incident illustrates the conflicting impulses at work in Stefano. On a very deep level he felt a need to be taken care of, to be fathered, and his continual slides into disarray were a way of ensuring that kind of attention. He kept tripping up because he needed to know that there was someone there to pick him up. The phone calls to Giovanni were a bid for that kind of attention. (And that he called Giovanni, a man whom he'd met that very day, on the night of his overdose indicates that he knew he couldn't turn to anyone in New York anymore—either because they were the cause of the problem or because he had imposed on them under similar circumstances once too often.) But once Stefano had gained the kind of support he seemed to crave, he rebelled against it and moved on. It was as if he were continually reacting to the pain of his father's death: searching for a substitute caretaker, then abandoning him, an act of aggression against a father who had deserted him.

Of his friends in Los Angeles, Stefano had remained closest to Sharon Kane. She had moved into a studio behind Chi Chi LaRue's house after her sabbatical in Venice following the excesses of the 1991 Miami White Party weekend. Kane was now making most of her income writing and recording music for gay videos and making the occasional guest appearance, often in a nonsexual role. Stefano would crash at Kane's apartment when he came to the West Coast, and indeed, *crash* had increasingly become the appropriate word. "Having Joey stay with you was like having a large horse in the apartment," Kane remembers. "He was just so overwhelming. He smoked, he was on the phone, he was ordering Pink Dot. He was big...his presence was big." He'd often be bingeing on drugs, and Kane would have to clean up after him. "I would come home and find him passed out, trashed, lying in a pile of Häagen-Dazs containers and cigarette butts," she says. "He'd wake up three days later." Despite the difficulties of his presence, she continued to put him up, forgetting from one visit to the next the trials his presence involved. "Sharon would be excited about Nick's visits," recalls Karen Dior, "and then after a few days she'd be sick of it. He would take over the apartment. He would be on the phone all the time, calling all over the world, racking up huge 976 bills. And he'd come and go at all hours, bringing people home with him. She'd vow never to have him stay with her again, and then sure enough the next time he would."

But even more troubling to Kane than the difficulties of Stefano's presence was the increasing absence of their emotional bond. She had watched him grow up, and the changes it had wrought in him saddened her, though she understood the necessity for them. "I think Nick closed down more to protect himself," Kane says. "He had grown up, he wasn't a little boy anymore. It's almost like he got hardened; he had to protect his softness." The danger of that hardening was that it put up an emotional distance that became harder to cross; it blocked out attachments to both casual clients and good friends. "People wanted Joey to be this *thing,*" Kane adds. "Everybody wanted a piece of him, and he had to put up a wall. But he did that with [his friends] too as time went on."

During the summer of 1993, Kane began hearing from Stefano by phone almost every day. He was on the road dancing, and Kane knew from experience that that could be a lonely life. "He was hinting that he wanted more, he wanted some stability," Kane says. "He said he wanted to buy me a ring. It was sweet. I asked him why he wanted to do that, and it was difficult for him to discuss what it meant, so he decided instead that we'd go on a trip." Stefano had, in fact, once casually asked Kane to marry him; though tempted, she didn't think it would be a good idea. But she could tell that Stefano now was anxious to be closer to her. "He was lonely, he wasn't happy," Kane continues. "I think he was having problems with his family; he felt like he needed a connection with somebody." He suggested a trip to Greece, and she agreed.

The trip got off to a bad start when the money he expected to receive for some work didn't arrive, and they had to depend on his credit card and Kane's cash. They stopped first in Paris, then Rome, where Kane hooked up with a friend who lived there. Whether it was caused by Stefano's jealousy of her taking up with a friend or was simply another of his quicksilver mood changes, Stefano, who had been eager to spend time with Kane, remained emotionally closed off. "He invited me on the trip, and then he was shutting me out. He wouldn't let me get close to him. He put up a wall, and it was driving me mad. I was angry." Kane had seen him act similarly before and had even discussed it with his other friends. But it was particularly frustrating that he'd gone as far as treating her to a trip to Europe to reaffirm their friendship, only to turn away from her once there.

From Rome they flew to Athens—with Sharon's friend in tow—where they spent a few days seeing the sights. After one night's festivities, Stefano abruptly decamped for Mykonos, their ultimate destination, leaving Kane, hungover, to follow later. Relations between Stefano and Kane had become strained, and when she arrived on the island, Kane and her friend camped out on one beach while Stefano remained in his condo near another, though Kane's friend soon left (though not before he too proposed marriage). Perhaps if she hadn't resisted Stefano's entreaties to join him in the condo, they might have repaired the damage to their fraying friendship. But Kane wanted to camp out, and life with Stefano on a Greek island—though he remained drug-free—was no less thorny than life with him in a West Hollywood apartment. "He was drinking every day, beer—and a lot of it," says Kane. "And he was obnoxious. People figured out who he was and tried to talk to him, and he would be rude and obnoxious. I couldn't stand to be around him." His irritation may have stemmed from the discovery that even halfway around the world, his Joey Stefano identity couldn't be escaped; on an Aegean beach as in Malibu, it was Stefano the porn star people saw, not Nick Iacona.

Kane made daily visits to Stefano's beach, but an island romp with him could be a hair-raising proposition. "I remember we rented motor scooters, and he crashed twice," Kane says. "He'd get drunk and drive it." Kane needed only one tour of the island on the back of a drunken Stefano's moped—

her heart leaping as they rounded corners giving way to steep cliffs—to remind her of the pleasures of her own beach. "And then he left the island," says Kane, who found that Stefano had departed and whose money had long since run out, leaving her without the resources to follow him. "He just decided he was going to leave, and he left. And I did not have a dime. I don't know if he knew that or not, but he had been paying for everything."

But Kane could be resourceful. Her journey from Ohio obscurity to porn stardom had been a woolly one and had included, to give just one sensational highlight, Kane's being held at gunpoint by her crazed ex-husband outside the mental institution from which he had just escaped. Being stranded without funds on Mykonos was hardly in the same league, though it posed some logistical problems. "I had to be creative," Kane says. "I went to the campsite and told them I didn't have any money to get off the fucking island, and I asked how much they'd give me for my tent and sleeping bag." They obliged her with enough cash to catch a boat to Athens and a cab to the hotel where she found Stefano, but it was not a happy reunion. Kane, of course, had not been pleased to be left without warning on the island; it was clearly an act of aggression on Stefano's part. He had probably been hurt by her choosing to spend so much time with her friend from Rome, making a mockery of the trip's unstated aim: to reignite their closeness. But rather than talk about his unhappiness, Stefano closed up, expressing his anger by abandoning Kane the way he must have felt she'd abandoned him. "After that I was pretty much fed up with him," says Kane. "We didn't even have a fight, really. You couldn't talk to him. We were not even communicating. I was ready to go home."

That was easier said than done on this ill-fated trip. At the Paris airport they went to the wrong terminal and arrived at the right one only to find that their flight was overbooked. Their tickets wouldn't be valid if they didn't make the flight, which, naturally, they didn't. They were utterly without funds—neither had so much as a single franc—and were at a loss at to what to do until Kane found a 100-franc note on the terminal floor. Stefano snatched it out of her hand, and they caught a taxi to a hotel in the city. They had to charge new tickets on Stefano's overburdened credit card and finally managed to leave for L.A. the next day.

"After that," says Kane, "it was kind of over." A trip that Stefano seemed desperately to need to solidify his closeness to Kane—it had, after all, been made in lieu of his giving her a ring, the traditional symbol of union—ended with a greater widening of the emotional gulf that had grown between them. For Kane, trying to reach Nick Iacona through the increasingly tough shell of Joey Stefano had become too draining. The effort rarely paid off in the kind of intimacy they once shared. "It was the drugs and the emotional closing-off," she says, explaining the reasons behind the cooling of their friendship. "I didn't want to live that way anymore, to feel like I was the one giving all the time, trying to pull him out of where he was..."

So Stefano had to return to his life, not with the emotional succor he had hoped to be able to draw on from an increasing closeness with Kane but with the knowledge that the hoped-for intimacy hadn't materialized, that he was as alone as he had been before. What was intended as a respite from the grind of dancing and tricking had been a grind of its own, a trip fraught with mishaps both practical and emotional. The emotional expense had almost matched the monetary one.

CHAPTER TWELVE

If 1993 marked the end of Stefano's close relationship with Sharon Kane, the last of the Los Angeles gang with whom he'd stayed in constant touch, it also marked the beginning of another friendship that would mean much to him. While dancing at the Gaiety that spring he met Alberto Shayo, and though their initial meetings were of the traditional escort-client kind, their relationship soon blossomed into something deeper, and Shayo proved to be a much needed resource—both financial and emotional—when Stefano found himself in desperate straits.

Born in Buenos Aires and trained as a dermatologist, Shayo had practiced medicine while pursuing as a hobby his passion for the artistry of the Art Deco period. Eventually his burgeoning work as an art dealer, which kept him on the road much of the time, began to conflict with his practice, and he had to choose between professions. Dealing in facial blemishes, noble though it is, was naturally no match for dealing in the refined beauties of Art Deco china and glass, and Shayo gave up his medical practice to pursue a full-time career as an art dealer. He established himself as an expert in sculpture of the Deco period, authoring the 1993 book *Chiparus: Master of Art Deco,* published by Abbeville Press. Soft-spoken and elegant, he had lived in Manhattan since 1987, in a small but handsome apartment in one of the posher stretches of 57th Street, just off Park Avenue. He travels frequently in his work, always accompanied by his roommate, Kita, half poodle, half Lhasa apso.

As might be expected from one whose life's work is the appreciation of beauty, Shayo had been an avid patron of the beauty on display at the Gaiety for several years, having become familiar with the establishment even before moving to New York. When he met Stefano that spring of 1993, he was moderately familiar with his work and knew that he had been one of the bigger names in the porn spectrum. "I was excited," says Shayo. "You know—'Ooh, the star! Here he is...' But he was not snobbish, not aloof. I approached him, talked to him, and we agreed to meet later." They had a mutually satisfying encounter, which was followed by several more. Shayo gave Stefano his number, and Stefano would call when he was in town; casual tricks turned into more protracted visits, with Stefano spending the day at Shayo's apartment, arranging dance gigs and catching up with friends in marathon phone sessions. They went to dinners and to movies, still Stefano's favorite pastime. It was all, of course, on Shayo's dime, but the relationship expanded from a simple sex-for-pay transaction to a more fluid friendship, a less rigidly mercenary relationship more akin to an artist-patron bond. Shayo provided support when needed, and Stefano worked his art, which was, of course, sex.

By now Stefano had moved out of his New York apartment and was depending on a shifting circle of friends for his shelter. Shayo joined that list, and every few weeks or months Stefano would announce his arrival, clambering out of a taxi with "seventeen shopping bags, all with dirty clothes." More often than not he'd arrive without a dime and call Shayo from the foyer of his apartment building requesting taxi fare. The taxi fare was no problem, but Shayo had to admonish him to dress a little more decorously than usual when visiting. His hair now down to his shoulders and usually pulled back in a ponytail, his body as beautiful as ever despite the chemical wear and tear, Stefano would be a rather startling apparition waltzing into Shayo's apartment building's sleek marble-and-glass foyer clad only in skimpy running shorts and tennis shoes. His was not a look often seen in Shayo's neighborhood.

Although he came to know Stefano better than most of Stefano's other escort clients, Shayo was certainly not the first to play an important role in his life. Talking to the *Gay Video Guide* in 1991, when dancing and escort work were less a necessity than a handy way of supplementing his video work, Stefano spoke candidly about the advantages escort work could bring his way. "I had some people who offered to fly me to Paris, Morocco, and Rome, but I canceled out and didn't go. See, I didn't take advantage of all the things that this business has to offer because I didn't want it all. I didn't want to travel all around the world doing escort work. I don't want the business to become my entire life. It's too much, doing the movies and escorting. In the beginning I didn't like doing the escort work 'cause it brought back too many bad memories of when I did tricks for drugs. But now I'm comfortable with escorting because I can pick and choose who I'm with. I've made some good friendships with some of my clients, and later down the line, if I ever get into a bad situation, I know that these people will help me. I have friends that will fly me here and there, and it's nice having them for support and not having to constantly work for it." As time went on and his video offers became fewer and farther between, it was the escort work that had to pick up the slack. He was indeed flown here and there, by clients from Florida, Texas, even Mexico. And he was not being blasé when he talked about not really wanting to travel the world; he was never a sophisticate, and when a client took him on a trip to Paris, Stefano proved impervious to the city's artistic treasures. He wrote postcards to Sabin and Mickey Skee detailing his boredom, the gist being, according to Skee: "'All he [Stefano's benefactor] wants to do is go to these stupid buildings and look at these stupid paintings on the walls.'" The Mona Lisa? "It was just a stupid painting," Skee says. "Joey was more interested in checking out the curators."

For many gay porn stars, escort work acts as a sort of retirement program. Who needs an IRA when your looks and sexual prowess, as amply demonstrated on video and in person, can capture the attention of a wealthy man willing to make an investment to take his favorite off the market? A certain famous composer keeps his pick in a swank L.A. apartment. Other performers are kept by less high-profile but equally solvent men and spend their days at the gym keeping their assets in trim. Stefano most certainly could have come to some such arrangement with one of his regular clients, but he had a need to be independent. "He had met a thousand and one people and had a thousand offers," says Shayo, to whom Stefano had opened up about his life and career. "But he was very independent. He didn't want to be attached." His peripatetic lifestyle wasn't just a necessity imposed by his work, it also expressed his need to remain in motion, to be free of encumbrances. "I don't want to be taken care of," he had told *Man-shots* magazine when he was starting out. "I want to do it on my own. I don't want a rich daddy to support me." He maintained a certain integrity in not settling down with a rich patron for purely financial reasons; but that didn't mean he didn't hope to find a haven in the love of someone he cared deeply about. The paradox at the core of his life may have been that he was constantly searching for a sense of security, of home, but turned away from it whenever it seemed within reach, remaining in motion when there is security only in stasis. His perpetual motion was a way of turning away from hope of happiness before it could turn to ashes, always abandoning rather than risking being abandoned.

Stefano had been working and playing in Florida since the beginning of his career, and as it became clear that New York was no more a salubrious environment for him than Los Angeles had been, he decided to move to South Beach. Doug Smith was still living in nearby Hollywood with his parents, and Stefano was impressed that Smith was continuing to pursue an education while holding an unglamorous if steady job in a convenience store. He had known Smith to be as drug-dependent as he was and took heart from the fact that Smith had been on a more or less even keel since getting out of prison in the summer of 1991. Perhaps Stefano too could make a break from the increasingly wearying cycle of drug binges as well as the circuit of dancing and tricking that it was becoming harder and harder to endure without the numbing effects of the drugs. He had a friend in Miami who had agreed to move in with him.

Stefano called Smith in September 1993 and told him about his plan to get out of New York, asking if Smith would fly up and help him move his things out of storage and drive a rented truck back down to Florida. Stefano had found a sponsor for his big move in an escort client who was a doctor from San Antonio, Texas; he had agreed to foot the bill. The doctor wasn't enamored of the idea of trucking down to Florida, so Stefano needed Smith to perform that function. In addition, the clean break hadn't begun yet, and Stefano was laying in a store of drugs to make the move less stressful. After assurances that the doctor would pay his rent for a month and foot the bill for the move, Smith agreed and flew up to New York a few weeks later. The night before the big move, Stefano and the doctor and another friend went to see Bette Midler at Radio City, and Stefano took his sponsor on a detour to the drug dealer, where they loaded up on Special K, crystal, and other substances. The next morning Stefano gave Smith a supply of the crystal to fortify him for the trip, and Smith hit the road, "stopping in every bathhouse on the way," he says, before arriving in Florida a day later.

He had expected to come home to a message from Stefano on his phone machine, since Stefano and the doctor should have beaten him back; they were flying, after all. The call he finally received from Stefano was collect, from the Tampa, Florida, city jail. In a spectacularly stupid move that can be attributed only to some odd impulse to thwart his own attempt to break away (although, of course, it could also be caused by a sufficient amount of Special K), Stefano had been unable to resist the urge for a cigarette on their flight. Carefully contravening the flight attendant's warning about tampering with the smoke detector in the bathroom—a warning, it must be said, that seems designed to plant the idea in nicotine-addled brains—Stefano had done the tampering and received the threatened punishment. He was arrested when the flight stopped in Tampa. In addition, a strip search revealed a cache of Special K on his person, and he was now facing those charges too. Exit the good doctor, who hopped on a plane to Texas forthwith, leaving Stefano to his own resources.

Stefano implored Smith to go to Tampa to help him out, offering as enticement the cache of drugs the doctor had secreted in an airport locker. Smith, whose keel was not so resolutely even after all, went to the rescue, finding Stefano petulant and utterly astonished that he had been incarcerated for three days. Without the money to make bail, Stefano turned to Shayo back in New York, asking him to wire money. Shayo came through, to the tune of $2,000 on October 19 and another $3,000 two days later. It was a remarkably generous gesture, and Stefano recognized it as such. He was moved to tears when Smith told him Shayo had sent the money without question. Stefano had been used to receiving sums of money—but it was always for services rendered. The arrangement with the doctor had been predicated on the idea that the doc would call the shots. That Shayo had sent such a large sum without getting anything in return touched him deeply.

Out on bail but somewhat dispirited by the ordeal, he met with a lawyer, who arranged to represent him at an upcoming hearing (Shayo again supplied the deposit). He followed Smith (and the drugs) back to Miami and moved into an apartment with his friend Art as arranged, though the doctor's deposit on one apartment had been lost and they had to find another. As with his trip to Greece with Sharon Kane, everything seemed to have gone wrong with his move south, and the pattern continued. After a month, Art decided he didn't want to live with Stefano after all, which hurt Stefano, whose move had been inspired partly by the idea of again having someone to live with. (He had begged Smith to move to New York to live with him when he first took up residence there, and eventually another friend had moved in.) Nor had there, in truth, been any attempt to break his drug habit. Indeed, though Stefano had left New York, New York soon came to him in the person of his friends from the city, who again descended on Miami for White Party weekend. The drugs, as usual, flowed freely. To keep himself solvent, Stefano set up dancing gigs at several clubs in both Miami and Key West, still a gay resort mecca. Smith acted as his booker.

But as November turned to December—the time of year when thoughts of his father's death and his birthday began to fill his mind—he retreated into drugs. "I started seeing the really messy side of his using," Smith recalls. "He would shoot up Special K intravenously. He wanted to be immobilized, to be out of it. I remember walking down a stairwell in an apartment building where he'd just bought drugs, and he couldn't wait to do it. He shot up immediately and collapsed right there on the stairway. I had to sit there with him. Blood was dripping all over the place. People were walking by. I was telling them, 'Don't worry…' I couldn't understand why he would do that."

He was freebasing cocaine for two weeks before a planned trip to New York at the end of December, Smith recalls. Although Stefano had been dancing regularly and Smith knew he'd been making good money because he'd made the bookings, when he arrived to take Stefano to the airport, Stefano had no cash.

In New York, a few days after Christmas, Stefano called Shayo. It was clear to Shayo, as his bankbook attested, that Stefano was a young man in trouble. When they met, Shayo asked him to lay out his problems; Stefano told him about the upcoming charges in Tampa, plus previous charges in that same city stemming from an earlier charge of lewd conduct, when he had been arrested during a performance at a club. He said he owed money to various lawyers and associates. "Nick, what do you need to straighten out your life? How much?" Shayo remembers asking. "He told me $3,000. I thought he could settle his debts, things would be OK, and he'd move on." They arranged to see the film *Mrs. Doubtfire* the next day, and when they met, Shayo gave him the money. What he had remained utterly ignorant of was Stefano's drug use.

On New Year's Eve—the night before he would turn twenty-six—Stefano checked into a Days Inn in Manhattan. Smith, working at the gas station convenience store in Florida, was paged at about midnight. He returned the call from the Days Inn and was put through to Stefano, who said he'd called to say good-bye: He had just slit his wrists. Smith hung up and called the hotel back, informing them that a guest had just sliced up his wrists in one of their rooms. In surreal fashion, they informed him that they really couldn't do anything about that—they weren't allowed to bother the guests. "I had to go through two or three people to get a manager before they'd do anything," Smith recalls. An ambulance was summoned, and Stefano was rushed to the hospital.

Shayo got a call from the hospital in the early hours of the morning and hurried over. Stefano lay in bed in a hospital gown. His wrists were wrapped in bandages brown with dried blood. He began crying when he saw Shayo, saying, "I'm sorry. I burnt off the $3,000." It was heartbreaking that he thought Shayo would be more distressed at his having lost the money than at his having tried to kill himself. It's a sad indication that his years of selling sex had made him see all his relationships as mercenary rather than personal. "He kept crying and told me how nobody had taken care of him," Shayo says. "He felt he was washed up, his star status was fading. He felt that people used him, wanted Joey Stefano but didn't want to know who was behind that." Shayo, of course, assured him that he didn't care about the money, that indeed he did have people who cared about him, and said he wanted Stefano to get back on his feet. He brought him back to his apartment that morning. His injuries weren't serious enough to require hospitalization. Shayo was devastated to realize that his attempt to help Stefano with money had gone only to feed him drugs. He felt somehow responsible and wanted to help him turn himself around. Stefano stayed with Shayo for the next few days, and one morning Shayo sat him down and asked him to write down what was bothering him: "I said, 'Write down your problems. Let's try to talk about them— let's try to solve them.'"

Stefano took a pen and a yellow writing pad and wrote the following:

No job.
No money.
No self-esteem.
No confidence.
All I have is my looks and body,
and that's not working anymore.
I feel washed-up.
Drug problem.
Hate life.
HIV-positive!

At the bottom was a slash, which may have been used to underline either just the bottom line or the list in its entirety.

What sad simplicity it has, just thirty-two words scrawled by a man who had just turned twenty-six. There is nothing spectacular here, no exotic sources of anguish: It's a litany of depression's most reliable sources, a stream of annoyances most can easily understand. Many gay men may feel a deep sympathy with more than one or two of Stefano's succinctly stated griefs—and some may identify with the whole damned list! They bespeak a profound despair born of the sometimes baleful meeting of personality and circumstance.

"No job. No money." These, of course, are circumstances that people face every day without succumbing to suicidal thoughts. It's telling that Stefano clearly didn't consider the work he continued to do—dancing, tricking, making the occasional video—as a job. Although in his first interview with Sabin, for *Thrust* in 1989, he had said modestly, "I don't consider being a porno star some big deal. To me, it's a job, and I'm having fun," unlike many other of his fellow performers, Stefano had never really treated it like an occupation. He had entered the business as a starstruck kid and remained one. He did it for the sex and because he could make money at it, but he never took it seriously as a profession. Whether it was because at heart he bought into the idea that having sex for a living was a shameful habit and not really a job at all or because his ability to earn a living at it was wavering, Stefano obviously thought he didn't have a profession.

In addition, of course, there was the large strike against his self-esteem that he shared with all gay men and women: Though they may harbor no thoughts of inferiority on an intellectual level for being gay—or have learned to cast such thoughts aside—homosexual men and women grow up in a society that telegraphs its official disdain for homosexuality every day, in every stratum of society, from earliest childhood through adolescence and on into adulthood. And Stefano certainly didn't grow up in a family, or a social milieu, that held sophisticated views about the subject. "Back where I come from," he told an interviewer in 1990, "gay life is not very popular, it's not accepted.... I had problems with drugs and drinking, and I was in a program for two years." It's clear from his yoking the two phenomena together that one influenced the other: His drug problem was in some ways a reaction to the pain he'd felt growing up gay in a world that sneered at it. He eventually grew to glory in being gay and had the strength of nerve to make a career of it, but he was as aware as any gay man or woman is that he was part of a minority viewed with suspicion or hatred by large segments of society. It is not a condition that increases feelings of self-worth.

Nor, in the end, did his work in the sex business seem to have given his self-esteem a boost. He was revered for his beauty, but it was a double-edged sword. The attention his looks had gained made them play an unnaturally large role in his feelings of self-worth. The more the beautiful body named Joey Stefano was worshiped, the less value the boy inside the body seemed to have. A dependence on physical appeal for his livelihood bred a preternatural fear of losing those looks to the rigors of age. As Stefano's note so clearly states, even at twenty-six, as beautiful as he'd ever been, he already thought he could feel the cold touch of time dimming his prospects, casting a pall over his future. From his dependence on it, he came to believe that he was his beauty, and if that failed, there was nothing left: "All I have is my looks and body, and that's not working anymore."

Jerry Douglas tells a fascinating story that illustrates just how central Stefano's sexual appeal was to his ego. A few years after making *More of a Man,* he and Stefano were having dinner in New York, and the conversation got around to the subject of Stefano's appeal. "I said, 'You know, Joey, I think you're a beautiful man, but I have no desire and never have had any desire to go to bed with you,'" Douglas recalls. "I'll never forget the look on his face. He was crestfallen. He was stunned that someone might not want to respond to his charisma. A cloud seemed to pass over his face. He said, 'You don't?'" But his dismay gradually turned to pleasure. "He suddenly realized that I liked him as a person and not as a potential sex object," Douglas continues. "It was a wonderful moment. He just couldn't believe that someone was immune to his charms, because that was what he had traded on all his life."

The idea that his sexual appeal was "not working anymore" may have been partly delusional—he was still getting regular dance gigs and had shot several videos in 1993—but in a sense Joey was "washed-up" in the business in which he was once a top star. His video earning power had long since peaked.

Behind the recklessness, weaving in and out of Stefano's life like a doppelgänger he couldn't shake, was his drug problem. Did the drugs cause the problems or the problems cause the drug use? The answer is probably both. Stefano had learned to depend on their easy promise of escape in his mid teens, at the time of his father's death and his awakening sexuality. Though he had gotten clean in Philadelphia before moving to L.A., once there he was unable to resist the appeal of drugs just as he was unable to resist indulging his huge appetite for sex. The drives weren't unrelated: Stefano was addicted to the moments of oblivion that only sex and drugs could supply. He knew his drug use was a "problem," but he was never serious about finding a solution. It was easier to stop for a while if you knew that you could always go back, and it was easier to go back if you knew you could stop for a while. He didn't see that that was a cycle as dangerous as permanent addiction.

Finally there was that last item on his list of woes: "HIV-positive," the ultimate problem if we choose to see his list in ascending order of importance, and the only plaint that rated an exclamation point. Although in brief talks with friends he seemed to indicate he'd come to terms with it, Stefano often was most quiet about his deepest concerns, and the note, written when he had let his defenses down, illustrates that it was, after all, a prime concern. It threatened the beauty that was central to both his livelihood and his self-esteem, and it put a question mark over his future, making it that much harder to kick his drug habits.

Shayo was, of course, overwhelmed by the knowledge of the depth of Stefano's problems, the desperation he felt. In the days that Stefano spent in his apartment after the suicide attempt, they talked at length about how Stefano could cope with the issues he'd raised. "He felt his problems were mounting," Shayo says. "I think he had lost his course. He wasn't going toward anything. I tried to give him hope, to tell him that not all doors are closed, that he had people who cared for him." Shayo took him to the doctor and the dentist. At the doctor's office, after being told of Stefano's drug problems, the doctor looked pointedly at Stefano and asked, "What do you want?" Recalls Shayo: "He avoided the question. The doctor asked again, 'What do you want?' His answer was short-term: 'To go to Miami, to get into an HIV program.' He never answered the long-term question." Shayo also wired money to a Tampa lawyer, who managed to clear the drug charge, since Special K, technically, is not a controlled substance.

Stefano's demeanor brightened gradually, and he decided to return to Philadelphia and stay with his sister for a few weeks, perhaps to find a job there. He was thoroughly burned out from the dance circuit and wanted to give it up for good. Smith packed up what Stefano had left in his Miami apartment and sent it to Philadelphia.

Although Shayo had come to care deeply about Stefano, he knew that he couldn't take responsibility for his life—and Stefano didn't want him to. Despite their new closeness, there was in their relationship a trace of difficulty stemming from the disparity between Shayo's world and Stefano's. They came from vastly different circumstances—Shayo from a well-to-do family in Argentina, Stefano from the lower-middle-class Philly streets—and a permanent relationship wasn't the answer to Stefano's problems. A few days after Stefano left, Shayo wrote in his diary his reaction to the events of the past week: "After a couple of hours I brought him home from the hospital, to rest, relax, recover his thoughts, talk.... His spirit is in disarray; he's insecure, scared, destitute. It was never my intention to control, manipulate, but, yes, to hold firm and give all I can, and more, too. This has been my nemesis. After five days he's back to his roots in Pennsylvania. It's a friendship that will last, but I fear for him. For his drug use, mainly. May he cling to simple things, caring and love; a job and sense of security will follow. As for myself, I cannot permit myself to fall in love. My barrier is up and my shield protects me well. I do feel deeply for him, perhaps because he's such a desperate case. There are no facades. 'Give a big kiss to Kita,' he said as he got on the train. I care for him more than I would like to admit."

CHAPTER THIRTEEN

It was obvious that Stefano felt great gratitude for Shayo. Shortly after his arrival in Philadelphia, Stefano wrote him a letter, postmarked February 4, 1994:

Al,

I don't know where to start. Everything is fine. I'm really starting to see the light. I'm scared but that can't stop me. I miss Kita and you, so I'm throwing a big kiss to you. I can't wait to start work so I can not have all this time on my hands. I can't tell you how much you helped me. Thank you for being my friend. Right now all I can say is thank you for helping me out. Once I start working and getting on my feet I can start paying you back. I hope you do well in Paris. In the next few months I'm gonna start sending money.

Love, Nick

But work didn't materialize in Philadelphia. Stefano had hoped to find a job in the construction industry; he had told friends he had held a construction job previously. (One also wonders whether a fetish for construction workers might not have been at work. It was like him to be attracted to the über-macho construction milieu, so often exploited in fantasy by the porn industry.) In the end, a hoped-for connection fell through, and Stefano spent his time helping his sisters, Linda and Tina, take care of Linda's children. He had always been good to his three nieces and nephew, always thinking of them at Christmastime and particularly looking forward to spending time with them.

His relationship with his sister Linda had had its ups and downs. When he started out in the adult-film industry, he told Sabin in the *Thrust* interview that he hadn't apprised his family of his burgeoning career. It's obvious that the world of his sisters in Marcus Hook, Pennsylvania, was considerably removed from the porn business: He could begin appearing in videos and magazines without worrying that his sisters and mother would be likely to find out. Asked if his family knew about his work, Stefano said, "My mother doesn't know, and my dad's dead. I have one younger sister, one older, and they don't know I'm gay. For me, right now, they don't need to know. If they find out or one of my friends finds out, then I'll have to deal with it. I don't think my family would be able to deal with it. They had a lot of expectations for me and point to someone else and say, 'That fag.' No, I'm not ready to let my mother know."

But as he started to earn significant sums of money, Stefano began sending money home to his sisters, and he took pride in being able to treat the whole family to trips to the Jersey shore, to a limousine ride here and an Atlantic City jaunt there. "I think because his father had died that he sort of felt he had become the man of the family," says Kane. "I think he felt a great responsibility for his family. He sent them money, tried to help them out. But he had a hard time telling them he was gay *and* a porn star *and* HIV-positive." He eventually opened up about his unorthodox occupation, however, so his continuing generosity to his family (even when he himself was scrambling to make ends meet) may have been an attempt to justify himself in their eyes, prove that his work—and thus he himself—was worth something. It was clear to all his friends that his relationship with his family was at times a very difficult one. Shayo recalls protracted and rancorous phone conversations whose subjects Stefano would refuse to disclose. Adds Kane: "When you would start to talk to him about his family, there were so many knots, so many tangled emotions. I feel that that was the root of his problems. Not that it's their fault, but he was never able to get in there and sort it all out. It haunted him."

So if Stefano often returned to his sisters' side when he needed a respite from the frenzy that sometimes overwhelmed his life, theirs was not a world he felt completely at home in either. The ghost of the young man who had had to hide his deepest feelings from his family rose before him when he returned to visit his hometown, as it does for many gay men and women. So did the specter of the "expectations" his family had for him, which surely did not include gay-porn stardom and drug problems. They were uncomfortable ghosts to live with. Shayo, who had been sending Stefano care packages of food and small sums of money—he knew now the danger of large ones—went to Philadelphia for a weekend, and Stefano joined him in his hotel. "I asked him how he was doing," says Shayo, "and though he was happy with his family, he wanted to move on."

But how and where to move on?

When the construction job fell through, Stefano began casting around for other ideas, calling Smith constantly, "saying, 'What kind of job am I gonna get?'" Doug remembers. "I said, 'Girl, I started out in a gas station as a clerk in the store. If you want to do that, you've got to make that decision.' He didn't want to dance anymore."

But the effort to find a new path for his life once again proved too difficult, despite his dramatically expressed disenchantment with it. He left Philadelphia and by spring was back in New York, dancing at the Gaiety.

It's easy to dismiss Stefano's inability to break free from the lifestyle he'd come to abhor as simple weakness, a laziness of spirit. But changing careers isn't easy for anyone, particularly in the '90s, an era of reduced opportunity and increasing competition. Five years in the sex industry had not equipped him for any other work. It took a kind of confidence he lacked to reimagine a life for himself outside the field he'd found success in, just as it takes a certain amount of courage for the insurance company executive to give up his career track after five years of experience to start afresh in the film industry or in social work. For many people, the job taken just out of college to pay the bills becomes a permanent occupation by default, as circumstances conspire to reinforce life's status quo. So it was for Stefano. He had had the luck to be successful at a job that he'd enjoyed, but when he grew disenchanted with it, he found he was trapped in it by the force of circumstance and the easy money it continued to offer. He didn't seem to have a choice.

In Los Angeles the news of Stefano's suicide attempt had been filtered through the industry rumor mill, reaching print in the form of an item in Dave Kinnick's "Secrets of the Porn

Stars" column in the *Advocate Classifieds* magazine. Kinnick wrote for the February 22, 1994, issue:

> Got a call bright and early the first Monday of 1994. It was one of our editors. Seems he had received two different phone calls on his office answering machine over the weekend asking if *The Advocate* was planning to run an obituary on Joey Stefano any time soon. It seems a rumor was going around to the effect that it might be a good idea.
>
> One of the callers was local and identified himself only as one of Joey's fans. The other was in the video industry but based in Northern California. What to think? We called up one of Joey's director-friends, who called up a performer-friend, who called up a friend-friend and asked if she knew how Joey was doing. The answer was, "He's fine. We just got back from seeing a movie. Why?" So much for the rumor. For the record: Joey Stefano is not at all dead.
>
> But it started us wondering just how pervasive was the "Joey's dead" story before it got squashed here? Is it going to be like the time everyone was saying that Paul of the Beatles was deceased after he appeared on the *Abbey Road* album cover barefoot? After all, Stefano works barefoot quite often. A rumor like that could become unmanageable awfully quickly in his kind of situation. We hope Joey will live on for many, many new years....

Gino Colbert read the item with a mixture of puzzlement and foreboding. Like most of Stefano's other L.A. friends, he would hear from him when he was coming through town and looking for work. But months might go by between contact, and Stefano was constantly on the move, making it impossible to find him to get to the bottom of the rumors. As it happened, a week after reading Kinnick's column, Colbert heard from a dancer who was working at the Gaiety with Stefano. "I said, 'Do me a favor: Go into the dressing room, drag Nick to the pay phone, and call me collect,'" Colbert recalls. "It was the first time I had talked to Nick in a year. He told me he had been on crack, had become really addicted, gotten off, was living with his sister in Philly. I told him that one of the movies he'd done had gotten great reviews, and I sent him a copy." They also made arrangements for Stefano to come out to L.A. to shoot again. That spring they made their last video together, *Tijuana Toilet Tramps,* whose priceless title alone places it among Stefano's better late films (though his scene was later cut into one of the worst ones, an execrable compilation movie called *Gay and Kinky*; while undeniably gay, the movie has nothing kinky about it, unless it may be considered kinky to have sex on a couch of such surpassing ugliness that a pair of Budweiser beach towels thrown over the arms constitutes an aesthetic improvement). Amusingly shot in a faux documentary style, *Tijuana* is one of the few porn movies whose cinema verité trappings are actually intentional. Despite the years of hard living, Stefano, with his hair almost to his shoulders, looks as sexy as ever, although there is an air of fatigue in his performance. Colbert recalls that Stefano was pleased with his costar, an individual of the beefy and ethnic variety, and expressed a desire to work with another of the cast members. Stefano was supposed to do the box-cover shoot but left town before it could be arranged. The video's original title, the more mundane *Toilet Trash 2,* gained its geographic twist when Colbert slated a couple of the vaguely Latino models in Stefano's stead.

But if Gino Colbert, an old friend, was happy to give Stefano work, others were less accommodating. Peter Scott, who had last heard from Stefano when he'd booked his Texas dance tour a year earlier, also got a call from him that spring. "He asked if I could get him some work," says Scott. "I started calling around to the film companies. I got absolutely no response. They weren't interested. I mentioned it to Falcon, to Catalina, to Studio 2000, to VCA, even Forum Studios. The gist was, 'Joey's old news; he's had it.' I didn't call him back to tell him that I couldn't get him a job digging a ditch."

In any case, at the same time that Stefano was going through the motions of scaring up more video and dance gigs, he was also planning once again to move himself to Miami and quit the gay porn lifestyle for good. And this time he had a new enticement: love.

Stefano had met the Cuban-born Alain Trigoura in South Beach during an extended visit during the summer of 1993. Trigoura, then 22, the son of a butcher, had been raised in Miami after leaving Cuba with his family at the age of 8. He was working a day job at the Ponce de Leon Mortgage Company when he met Stefano at the Warsaw Club, their eyes locking across the dance floor one night. Stefano approached Trigoura, and they danced; when Stefano took off his shirt, Trigoura noticed his distinctive tattoo and realized who he was. His twin brother had sent him an autographed photo of Stefano a few years before, and he was surprised to find himself dancing with the man in the 8-by-10 glossy. They made a date to go to the gym a couple of days later. Without the enforced intimacy of porn and escort work, Stefano reverted to his basic shyness. Trigoura too was quiet on their first date, but they began seeing each other frequently.

Stefano had been in town for an extended visit, and by the time it ended, Trigoura's job at the Ponce de Leon Mortgage Company had ended too; too many nights spent with Stefano had made it impossible to get to work on time. But he quickly found another job as a bellman at the Shore Club Hotel. Stefano hadn't worked much in the few weeks they'd spent together, and on the one occasion that he danced at the Warsaw, he insisted that Trigoura stay home. "He said he'd be embarrassed and nervous," Trigoura recalls. "My ex-roommate wanted to take pictures, and he wouldn't let her." Joey Stefano had been dancing in front of strangers to make a living for almost five years, but when a friend was in the audience, it became Nick Iacona up on that stage.

When Stefano left for a gig in California, he told Trigoura he was planning to move to Miami and wanted to continue their relationship. But once back in L.A., he appeared to have second thoughts and called Trigoura to tell him that he "just wanted to be friends. He didn't want to be with me," Trigoura recalls. Stefano again appeared to be succumbing to his instinct to protect himself by cutting himself off from someone he was afraid he'd care for too much. Or perhaps, as Trigoura says, he was "just playing games." (Or perhaps it amounts to the same thing.) Trigoura was puzzled but not offended and wrote Stefano a friendly letter to that effect.

As 1993 drew to a close, of course, Stefano did indeed make a move to Miami, but he was deeply involved in drugs and spiraling toward his suicide attempt. He didn't call Trigoura, perhaps because he didn't want to see him, perhaps because he was too caught up in his binge. When he retreated to Philadelphia to regroup, the two resumed contact.

With Stefano's return to New York had come a return to drug use. Caught up once again in the cycle that had only months before led to his suicide attempt, Stefano had a change of heart about his relationship with Trigoura: He called Trigoura and told him he was thinking of moving to Miami again, leaving it up to Trigoura to dictate his course. "He couldn't decide whether to come or stay away," Trigoura says. "He asked me if I would live with him, be his boyfriend, and I said yeah." Stefano was again looking to be taken care of—emotionally, at any rate—and Trigoura was the man for the job.

Things got off to a promising start. Stefano flew down in high spirits, and the two lived with a friend of Trigoura's before finding an apartment on Collins Street, one of South Beach's main drags, above the Sushi Rock Cafe. Stefano was adamant about wanting to find a steady job, and since Trigoura was looking to find a new one, they began going on job calls together. The South Beach boom was in full swing. Hotels and eateries were opening apace—Ian Schrager's ballyhooed Delano Hotel was one of the job calls the pair went on—and there were lots of service jobs available that wouldn't have required extensive experience. Stefano and Trigoura had hoped to find jobs together—it certainly would have made things easier for Stefano—but it didn't pan out. Stefano's enthusiasm was crippled by a deep sense of insecurity, and he couldn't muster the will to persist in finding work. "He wouldn't call about the jobs after an interview. He wouldn't do it," says Trigoura. "He was too insecure. He would say, 'I don't think they're gonna hire me. All I've done is modeling. I have no qualifications.' I told him they would teach him."

Stefano also approached Smith about finding work. In fact, Smith arranged a job for him tending bar in Fort Lauderdale a few months before, but Stefano never showed up for work. He even asked Smith about getting him a job in the minimart where he worked. But Smith knew that was a scenario unlikely to come to pass. "I couldn't picture that he would ever really do it," says Smith, "even though he said he wanted to."

So Stefano spent his days with Trigoura watching soaps and going to the gym. When Trigoura went to his job at night,

Stefano would roller-blade over to visit him. But for Stefano, time on his hands was always a liability; it was more than likely to be filled with drugs. And, indeed, a month after moving in with Trigoura, he confessed that he was still fighting a drug problem. Trigoura hadn't been unaware of the fact: He had come home one day to find Stefano "lying on the bed looking weird" and unable to stand up. The floor was covered in shattered glass and water from a vase of flowers Stefano had knocked over on his way down.

Stefano told him he wanted to stop using and wanted to sign up for a Narcotics Anonymous program. He asked if Trigoura would go to the initial meeting with him, and Trigoura agreed. Stefano went ahead and made an appointment with a counselor, but when the hour came around, he turned to Trigoura and said, "Let's go to the gym." Trigoura was wary of pushing him into anything, so they skipped the appointment. A few weeks later Stefano's determination returned, and he made another appointment at NA. This time he begged off on an even flimsier pretext: He stayed home to watch a particularly compelling episode of *Days of Our Lives,* his favorite soap. His commitment to kicking his drug habit was obviously weak. Starting a new life in Florida, with the added burden of trying to make a relationship work—something he hadn't seriously attempted before—must have seemed too frightening to attempt without the escape valve of getting high. Knowing that Trigoura didn't like his drug use, he tried to keep it from him, but he continued to take Special K.

In other respects Stefano tried to make his relationship with Trigoura the perfect marriage. "He said I was the first man he'd loved," says Trigoura. "He said he was happier now than he'd ever been. You could see it in his face." Stefano liked to cook and would whip up chili or pasta almost every night.

Indeed, he seemed to take his new househusband métier quite seriously and lacked a housewife's equanimity in the face of a typical spousal spat: One afternoon he prepared lunch only to find that Trigoura wouldn't come to the dinner table—he was too engrossed in one of the soaps Stefano had gotten him hooked on. In a fit of rage, Stefano threw the food away.

But it was relatively smooth sailing for a while, and Stefano seemed to be finding a kind of contentment that had always eluded him. He talked about introducing Trigoura to his family and told his friends, in his marathon phone sessions, that he was happy to be in love at last. Trigoura too was happy, though his knowledge of the excesses of Stefano's past made him hold some of his emotion in reserve. "I would say he loved me more," says Trigoura, "because I was a little insecure about him. I thought he was too crazy, even though I didn't see that when he was with me. I was a little afraid to commit."

If Stefano's personal life was promising, his professional life remained troublesome. Halfhearted attempts to locate steady employment in Miami had, of course, not been fruitful. Even with Trigoura's support, he couldn't muster the confidence to pursue attempts to find alternative work, and he had to support himself with the occasional trick or dance gig in Miami or Key West. He swore to Trigoura that he wanted nothing more to do with the porn-star lifestyle, but he had to keep earning a living. It was clear to Smith, who was still booking dance gigs for him, that his desire to quit the business was genuine. Stefano was so tired of the routine that he required significant infusions of drugs to be able to perform. "At clubs the only time he was really messy was when he had to perform," Smith says. "I'd drive him down to Key West, and he'd get all fucked up, barely make it, and then want me to drive him right home."

Indeed, that cracks were beginning to show in the new serenity of his life became apparent as his drug habit continued to increase. He'd now switched from Special K to heroin and was struggling to keep his indulgence from Trigoura. "I remember going to get heroin, and Nick would want to shoot up right away before Alain got home," says Smith. "He'd tell him we'd gone to a movie when we went to get drugs."

Needing to make a significant sum of money for a planned trip to the shore with his family, Stefano booked a dancing gig at San Francisco's Campus Theater. It was the first time he'd been on the road in months, and Trigoura remembers that he wasn't pleased about going. Though he had been supporting himself with occasional dance dates in Florida and had been to New York once since moving to Miami, those gigs could be written off as minor and necessary bumps on the road to a new life. But the California trip was different: He'd be flying all the way to the other coast, leaving behind for at least a week his new lover and the cozy domesticity he'd strenuously been trying to establish. He'd be thrown back into the old lifestyle without the safety net of Trigoura or Shayo to turn to if he felt himself coming apart at the seams. But he wanted very much to treat his mother and sisters to a vacation at the beach, and if he could just manage to hold on to his money this time, he would have the trip to look forward to.

Knowing he was going to be in San Francisco for a week, Stefano had been in contact with Steven Scarborough, the former production manager and vice president of Falcon Video, who had started his own company, Hot House Entertainment, a few years earlier. Scarborough was creating a series of videos featuring interviews with porn stars as a kind of oral history of the business. He had wanted to tape a session with Stefano because he felt that Stefano had had a significant impact on the business. In trying to get in touch with Stefano, he'd discovered the dire tatters of his reputation: His camera-man couldn't believe Scarborough was interested in using someone who was widely reported to be a mess and more or less washed-up. But Scarborough persisted, knowing that Stefano had been a one-of-a-kind presence in the business. "In a restaurant, if you walked in with him, people turned and looked," remembers Scarborough. "Even in a straight restaurant, where people didn't know who he was. He had something about him that people noticed. A lot of it was about sex, of course, but he also had that thing that makes people stars. And there was a bit of a tragic air about him; there was something that made people want to reach out and help him.

"I've worked with smarter guys, better-looking guys, guys who worked it harder, who actively promoted themselves, who did all the right things, who didn't get negative press, who had huge dicks and were tops. But against all the rules he was one of the icons of this business, and he'll stand the test of time."

Eventually he and Stefano caught up with each other, and they made arrangements to do the video when Stefano was in town for the Campus gig. Scarborough hadn't worked with Stefano for five years, since the beginning of his career, when Scarborough had directed him in two of his three Falcon videos. He had followed Stefano's career and had attempted to book him for video shoots on a few occasions since those first shoots, but circumstances—or Stefano's scattered life-style—had kept them apart. "There was a period in the '90s when I thought he was not employable for the kind of movies I was making," says Scarborough. "He was overexposed, and he was a mess. It was too much of a risk for us. I work with up-and-up people, don't want any drugs around. It's a business. We start at 7:30 or 8 in the morning so we can be done at 6, rather than in L.A., where they start at 2 or 3 and work till midnight. With Nick you never knew where he was going to be. The other question was always, Is he going to be on drugs? He knew that if he showed up and wasn't in good shape, I would send him away. That may have been why he flaked out on a couple of shoots with me over the years."

Scarborough was preparing for the experience of working with Stefano again with some trepidation, as would be expected, and though Stefano showed up as scheduled the day before the video shoot to do a still-photo session, Scarborough, who was out of the Hot House offices running errands, got a warning call on his car phone from his bookkeeper soon after Stefano arrived. "She said, 'Steven, I think you should come back here. I can smell junk a long way away, and I know this boy is not clean. They're having trouble upstairs.'" Scarborough duly returned to the office and marched into the studio, where the relatively inexperienced photographer was indeed having a difficult time with Stefano. Scarborough asked him flatly if he was on drugs: "Are you or are you not fucked up?" was how he recalls putting it. Perhaps knowing a kernel of truth would hide the worst, Stefano said he'd just taken a Valium earlier in the day because he'd been nervous about the shoot. Scarborough was most worried about the next day's video session and tried to get Stefano to agree to spend the night at the studio, where several rooms were often used to house models. He thought that would be the best, if not the only, way to keep him out of trouble. But Stefano begged off, saying he had some errands to run.

And when he showed up the next day, he was in fine form. The interview went smoothly. Among the topics covered most extensively, Scarborough remembers, was Stefano's family. He talked about having gone back to his sisters to regroup from the dancing and the hustling and the movies. He returned again and again to his upcoming plans to treat his family to a few weeks at the seashore. He'd already booked the house and was clearly excited about the trip; it was the whole purpose of his visit to California, he explained. He had managed to save the money he'd earned at the Campus and was ready to go home.

Indeed, he was so worried about spending the money he'd earned before he got back that he asked Scarborough to give him his money the next morning, just before he left for the airport. Scarborough again invited him to stay at the offices, since they were just a few minutes away from the airport, but again he refused, saying he had some business to finish up. But Scarborough offered to drive him to the airport, saying he'd send a runner to pick him up the next morning.

While Scarborough was at the bank the next morning getting cash to give Stefano his fee, he got a call from the runner he'd sent to find him. He had managed to locate Stefano and get him back to the offices, but Stefano was in a state that demanded Scarborough's presence. He rushed back to the office. Upstairs was a scene Scarborough describes as "tragic but humorous." Stefano was standing in the kitchen, surrounded by an astonished audience of staffers, vainly attempting to spread some apricot jam on a bagel—in itself an act that can only be explained as the result of extreme intoxication. And, indeed, he was clearly high, his voice an incomprehensible slur. Still, he seemed relatively functional, and Scarborough got him in the car, where he attempted to discover what had happened. Stefano blamed it on one Valium too many again, but it was clear that he was on something stronger. "He was mumbling and nodding out," says Scarborough. "I thought he was going to OD right in my car. He got me so flustered, I missed the freeway exit and was headed for downtown." Scarborough wanted to know what had happened; Stefano had seemed so together the day before, so upbeat. What could have happened? Barely able to find his voice, his emotions running so deep, even his drugged stupor couldn't disguise them, he told Scarborough that he had called his mother the night before and that she'd told him she couldn't go to the beach. "This kid was heartbroken," Scarborough says. "He had worked for this. He seemed to have a lot wrapped up in it. I think it was about seeking approval. It was hard to listen to. He had a knack for saying things that were so honest about himself—sometimes funny, sometimes sad. I could tell this really hurt." The drugs laid bare Joey's emotions, and Scarborough saw sitting beside him not a hard-living porn star but someone simple and sad, someone completely undone by what should have been a small disappointment. "He was really a damaged child," Scarborough adds. "I'll never forget it. My lover and I have talked many times about seeing him that last time, about how hurt he was, how wounded. That was how he was in life: a hurt child."

Scarborough sobered him up as best he could and got him to the airport. He never heard from Stefano again.

Back in Miami, Stefano's fragile stability seemed suddenly to shatter. His newfound domestic bliss had to a certain degree been a willful construction of his desperate need to be grounded, to find a shelter. Though he certainly loved Trigoura, it was clearly because he *wanted* to love him—needed to. Love was a card he hadn't yet played, an untried fashion of finding some peace in the world, a new device to shake free the demons that had haunted him since childhood. And suddenly it was all revealed to him as an illusion, a fantasy he'd constructed built on deception.

From the beginning Stefano had been attracted to Trigoura because he believed him to be bisexual. (Trigoura, for the record, denies this.) "The whole allure of Alain for Nick was that he was bisexual," says Smith, who recalls Stefano's coquettishly quipping, "My husband's straight." Stefano had always been attracted to straight men. It was an impulse that may have had its roots in his conflicted relationship with his father, a desire to recover in the love of a straight man the affection he missed from his father, who had died before the complexities of their relationship could be worked through. It was also an acting-out of his feelings of low self-esteem: He would pursue men he knew would be difficult to catch, because on some level he thought he didn't deserve to be loved. If he won them over, it would be an overwhelming proof of his worth.

In Trigoura, Stefano believed he had found the man who would make right all that had been wrong in his life. So when he discovered that his belief that Trigoura was bisexual was a false one, the jerry-built stability of his new existence was revealed as a fraud. Whether Trigoura actively fed Stefano's fantasy of him as bisexual—or even knew of it—isn't important. For whatever reason, Stefano believed it—and needed to believe it. When he discovered that it was a lie, he fell apart. Smith remembers him in tears over the subject, devastated and convinced that he'd been lied to. His perfect world had caved in, leaving him bankrupt. He turned to the one thing he'd been able to depend on, the only certain escape from his disappointment. He began shooting up heroin with a determination that startled Smith, who could see that Stefano was at a dead end. He halfheartedly asked Smith if he could move in with him. Smith was living in a small apartment in Hollywood, Florida, and agreed, though something told him Stefano would never take him up on it.

It was November, and Chi Chi LaRue's annual birthday bash was coming up. Stefano decided to go to L.A. for the event. Why not? He had suddenly lost his determination to quit the business. He had nothing to keep him in Florida anymore. His dream of a new life outside the life he'd come to know had evaporated. He bought a one-way ticket to Los Angeles.

CHAPTER FOURTEEN

Before making what would be his last trip to Los Angeles, Stefano placed the usual call to Sharon Kane, looking for a place to stay while he was in town. But Kane didn't want to play baby-sitter again. She was both working on her video sound-track commissions and living in the studio space behind Chi Chi LaRue's West Hollywood house. She knew that Stefano's presence would disrupt her routine. Kane had also heard through a mutual friend that he had begun shooting heroin again, and she didn't want to contend with the unpleasantness that was sure to cause. And in truth, since their unhappy trip to Greece the year before, Kane had maintained her distance from him—emotionally, at any rate—and wanted to keep it that way.

But she offered to help him find a place to stay, putting in a call to porn performer-director Crystal Crawford, the latest drag queen to follow LaRue's lead and parlay a way with a wig into a career in skin flicks. ("These days anybody who's a drag queen thinks they can direct movies," LaRue is fond of quipping.) Crawford is a somewhat controversial figure in the gay-porn *monde*—some would say he has more than just man trouble in common with the icon whose surname he adopted, Joan Crawford. He would be the first to agree, seeing numerous parallels in their sagas. "She was disciplined, her career came first. I'm disciplined in public with my demeanor," says Crawford. "We have the same problems with men—men pull me away from my career. She was a mainstream actress, and I do porn, obviously—but we've had similar setbacks. I've cut men out of pictures before," he concludes, adding as an afterthought, "My dog is named Christina."

The lanky, angular Crawford left Indiana as Brian Malley, taking to the drag scene at L.A.'s Four Star with an admirable practicality: "Let's face it, I make a prettier girl than I do a boy." He saw what porn had done for Chi Chi LaRue and segued quickly—some would say in Eve Harrington fashion—from makeup man to director-producer for Planet Group, the company whose mass-produced product had changed the dynamics of the industry. He was happy to play host to Joey Stefano; though his reputation had dimmed over the years, Stefano's name was still among the most resonant in the gay-porn world. Crawford offered the extra room in his Spanish-style house, just steps away from LaRue's, that was often used by visiting models.

He also arranged to pick up Stefano at the airport the night of LaRue's party, but when he arrived at the terminal, he walked past Stefano once before recognizing him: Stefano had buzzed off the long hair that had been his trademark for the past year and a half and now wore his dark hair cropped military-short. Back at the house Crawford "flew into drag"; they were running late for the party. Stefano talked about his failed relationship with Trigoura, and Crawford got the impression that Stefano was coming to L.A. to escape.

At the party itself, held in a studio in the San Fernando Valley, Stefano was in a quiet but friendly mood. Most of his business acquaintances didn't know he was back in town, and there was general excitement at his presence. He talked to LaRue about video work, and LaRue agreed to use him in a scene the following Monday in a Mustang video for Falcon Studios. All noticed that his handsomeness seemed tempered by the years of living on the edge; dressed in black jeans and tank top, he was still striking, but as the last photograph of Joey, taken at the party, shows, he no longer had the glow of youth. His eyes squinting unevenly, a five-o'clock shadow adding to the mottled texture of his skin, Stefano looks like a fighter who's been in one bout too many. Equally striking to all who knew him was his casual sobriety. The word around town, cemented by Dave Kinnick's *Advocate Classifieds* column item, was that Stefano had fallen off the deep end. Yet here he was, drinking Coke and turning down offers of drugs.

He told Mickey Skee that he had stopped doing drugs, reiterating the point to Karen Dior when he offered Stefano some cocaine. Dior had been struggling with drug problems himself and had been "slipping" lately; he was happy to see that Stefano seemed to have conquered his problem. In fact, both the gay and straight adult-film industries had been jolted by the death that summer of Savannah. She had fought substance-abuse problems in the years before her death. The story was reported widely in the press and, of course, reinforced the idea that the industry was a soul-killing machine rife with drug abuse and desperation. LaRue, Kane, and others who had known Savannah had been inclined to reexamine their own habits.

When Crystal Crawford was getting ready to leave at 2 a.m., he sought out Stefano to tell him he'd leave the front door open and was surprised when Stefano said he wanted to leave too; from his reputation, Crawford had expected him to party well into the night. On the way home they dished the party, and Crawford reflected on the fact that Ryan Idol had again been the center of attention, surmising that Stefano had noticed too. "I think he realized that he wasn't the top man anymore; Ryan was at the party, and there was all this hype about his new movie, *Idol Country,*" says Crawford. "And Joey had worked with Ryan in his first movie, so I think he kind of felt that he had slipped." In the four years since Stefano and Idol had begun together in the business, Idol had managed to maintain his popularity—and his hefty price. He and his handlers had crafted his career carefully, and he continued to reap the rewards of that prudence. Stefano, by contrast, was broke and was getting ready to return to video work out of desperation, making far less than he had when he and Idol had worked together.

The next morning Stefano woke up to a sadly familiar dilemma: how to get some money. He had fled to L.A. in haste and had used up what money he had been making in Florida on a last, determined drug binge with Smith. The answer he came up with was also sadly familiar: hustling. But he had been out of the L.A. loop for some time and had no way of getting word out that he was back in town. One option was to put an ad in the gay paper *Frontiers.* He was by no means the only porn star to ply his trade in such a public forum, but it was a resource he hadn't needed to resort to during all his previous sojourns in L.A. When he was at the height of his porn fame, the clients had found their way to him; he hadn't needed to seek them out. Sitting with Crawford over coffee and soap operas, he puzzled out the new problem of composing a written description of his appeal. "What should I put? What should I put?" he needled Crawford, who was surprised to have to tell him that the only text necessary would be his name and a phone number. But the ad wouldn't appear for a week, and Stefano needed cash immediately, so he placed a voice-mail ad on a 976 phone system and began setting up tricks. Befitting such low-end marketing, his prices were considerably lower than they had been at the height of his fame: He was making between $200 and $400 a trick.

To Crystal Crawford and his roommate, Christian Murphy, it seemed that Stefano was happy spending his days going to the gym, visiting with friends, and turning tricks. They'd spend the evenings together, watching videos or going out to dinner. Stefano said he wanted to attend some Alcoholics Anonymous meetings and even managed to squeeze one into his schedule. One evening he confided to Crawford that he was HIV-positive, adding that his T-cell count was fine and he was feeling good. There was nothing to indicate that beneath his sober, sensible exterior was the desperate man who had attempted suicide less than a year before, who had been binge-ing on heroin just days before. Once again Stefano seemed to have turned on a dime from desperate and self-destructive to sober and sensible. Crawford, who had been worried about putting up with his notorious messiness, was relieved to find him so easy to get along with.

But in between tricks and trips to the gym, Stefano spent the next few days reestablishing contacts with old friends and associates, and he revealed a darker picture of his state of mind to them. He went to see *Interview With the Vampire* Wednesday afternoon with Gino Colbert, and afterward they met Colbert's production manager, Luca Norcen, for dinner at West Hollywood's French Market. Stefano was in a desperately unhappy mood—and an oddly reflective one—and unburdened to them thoughts about his career. "He was very sad, very bitter," remembers Norcen. "He talked a lot about his career. He was sad about it overall, saying he'd done a lot and made a lot of money, but given the chance, he would not do it again. He felt people had taken advantage of him, had used him up and thrown him away and in the end weren't there for him. He said if he had a second chance, all he wanted from his life would be a husband, a house, a regular job, a yard—an everyday, regular life someplace."

It's strange to remember that this was a man of twenty-six speaking. Most men of his age would, of course, still be looking forward to seeing those fairly modest needs fulfilled with at least a modicum of confidence; that Stefano thought he would have needed "a second chance" to achieve them illustrates the depth of his disillusionment. He clearly believed that it was somehow too late for him.

In retrospect his words have the ring of finality, of course, but at the time they were mixed with more mundane matters. He talked about going back to Miami, saying that he still loved Trigoura and was upset it hadn't worked out. Indeed, he spent a half hour in the card shop after dinner picking out a card to send to him. He and Colbert also discussed work, and Colbert agreed to cast him as soon as he could. In the past Stefano had discussed with Colbert the idea of directing videos, as several other porn stars, and indeed Colbert himself, had gone on to do. It was a way of extending a career in the industry after the marketability of one's image had faded. But Stefano's interest waxed and waned with his moods, and though Colbert was willing to help him get a directing gig, Stefano never pursued it seriously. Colbert did want Stefano to meet his boss at Leisure Time/Stallion Video; Stefano's videos for the company had been the top sellers, even well after the peak of his career. They made a date for brunch on Sunday, and Colbert invited his boss.

In a series of visits to Sharon Kane, who was just across the street from Crystal Crawford, Stefano again revealed his bleaker side. Rolling up a sleeve, he made a point of showing her his track marks. "I've been shooting up heroin," he said almost matter-of-factly. "It was almost like he was proud of them," she says. "I don't quite understand why he showed them to me, whether it was for attention...or something else. What could I say? With him, it didn't shock me too much." Stefano talked on these visits of feeling hopeless, of wanting to get out of the business. He said he couldn't face going on the road dancing again. Kane knew from experience the psychological toll it could take: "I know what kind of a life that is—having sex with people who want you to be that image, that porno thing. It was getting to him."

Kane gave him the best advice she could. She knew that the trap he was in involved the necessity of turning another trick or doing one more video to get by, while endlessly deferring other plans. She knew it took both formidable concentration and the financial wherewithal to escape the easy money the lifestyle supplied. She put it as strongly and plainly as she could: "I asked him three days before he died, 'Do you have anybody who's willing to support you? Get someone to support you while you go to school. Is there something you want to do?' He said he didn't know. I said, 'There's got to be something; you've got to find one thing, because you'll have to have that one thing to focus on to take you out of where you are.' He needed a light at the end of the tunnel."

She concluded with a bald statement intended to shock him into seriously reevaluating his life: "I said, 'If you don't do it, you're going to die.'"

And she remembers the words he used to sum up his self-image during their last visit: "He said he felt like an old hooker with a bad drug habit."

Literally speaking, of course, he was. But that this had become the bedrock perception of himself, the person he woke to in his mind's eye every morning, was the final, sad result of his losing battle with the demon of low self-esteem. He had been a much beloved uncle to his sister's children, a supportive brother to his sisters, a loyal friend to many, and a man whose beauty and talent for sex were celebrated and much appreciated. But because of the dark bent of his personality and the shape his life had taken, he had arrived at age twenty-six at the belief that the future held no hope of change, that his life was of no consequence, that his being alive was a small, unnecessary thing. Who, after all, would be expected to mourn a hooker with a bad drug habit?

On Thursday, Stefano went to the gym in the afternoon as usual, but when he came home several hours later, Crawford noticed he was acting strangely. His eyes were half open, and Crawford's roommate, Murphy, who had had experience with drug addicts, sensed that he was on something. Stefano went into the bathroom, and they heard the shower running. It ran for ten, then twenty, then thirty minutes; there was no response when they knocked on the door. Murphy kicked the door down. Through floods of steam Stefano could be seen slumped in the stall, a needle in each arm. Murphy pulled the needles out and, after checking to see that his vital signs were still in evidence, cleaned up the blood and got him out of the bathroom and onto a bed. Crawford put in a call to Kane, who knew the routine and told him that there wasn't much to be done. Stefano would come around eventually. He was conscious less than a half hour later and came into Crawford's bedroom, crying and apologizing only partially coherently. "I can't control it," he was saying. "I need help."

But the next morning he woke with no ideas of altering his routine. He didn't even refer to what had happened the night before. They passed the day as usual and in the evening went to a club in Hollywood, hosted by director-producer Sam Abdul, where Sharon Kane was performing. LaRue was there and noticed a cut above Stefano's eye. Stefano explained that he'd accidentally bumped his head in the shower. He didn't elaborate, but LaRue suspected there was more to the story. LaRue warned him that he needed to look good for Monday's shoot. The cut had better heal. That night Stefano again stuck to Coca-Cola and went home relatively early with Crawford.

On Saturday, Stefano and Crawford spent another uneventful afternoon and in the evening stopped at the video store, picking up *Mommie Dearest* and *The Birds,* and the liquor store, picking up the makings of strawberry daiquiris. Stefano mixed the drinks, and they flopped down in the family room for a while, trying to outdo each other in anticipating lines from *Mommie*. People familiar with substance abusers will note those daiquiris as a rather bad idea; the mild intoxication of alcohol can quickly dissolve resolutions to avoid other drugs. After a while Stefano got up to take a shower, leaving Crawford to trade lines with the movie for what seemed like an unnaturally long time. This time Stefano had left the door open. Crawford peeked over the shower door and saw a syringe in the shower caddy. Stefano was propped against the shower wall, completely unconscious, his skin wrinkled from the moisture. Crawford dragged him out and managed to get him on the couch. He tried to call Kane, not knowing quite what to do. Murphy wasn't home either. So Crawford waited for Stefano to come around, which he soon did. But he refused to talk about what he'd done or why he'd done it.

They watched movies for a while longer, with Crawford insisting that Stefano spend the night in his bed so he could make sure he didn't shoot up again.

Clearly Stefano had returned to the pattern of bingeing and abstaining at whim. His friends had become so familiar with it that they didn't see these drug episodes as anything extraordinary. "I was just so grateful—horrible as it was—that it wasn't me who had to take care of him, to clean up the mess," Kane says frankly. "I had done it too many times." She recognized from their talks the depth of Stefano's unhappiness, but his dark side had always been just beneath the surface; his aura of helplessness had been integral to his appeal. And he had been talking for years now of wanting to escape the business, of wanting to kick drugs. Their final visits left her with a sad, frustrated feeling of finality, even as Crawford's desperate phone calls seemed to illustrate that things were just as they always had been—and always would be. "When he left here, I felt like I'd given him everything, said everything I could say," Kane says. "I felt it had ended a long time before, really."

On Sunday morning Kane, Crawford, Stefano, and porn star Casey Jordan had brunch. Stefano wasn't particularly glum; he spent most of the time admiring men walking by on the Sunset Strip. Later that afternoon he visited LaRue at home, where they talked about the next day's shoot. LaRue hadn't heard about Stefano's bouts; Stefano had asked Crawford not to tell him. But LaRue suspected he had been doing drugs and asked him what he was taking. "As he would whenever he was in a denial period, he said, 'Larry, stop saying that! I'm not on anything!'" LaRue remembers. Trying another tack, LaRue asked again about the cut above his eye, now almost healed. "I hit my eye in Crystal's shower," Joey answered, adding by way of explanation, "The nozzle is too low." Although they would presumably be seeing each other the next day, the visit ended with an odd gesture of finality on Stefano's part. "He came over and hugged me and kissed me and told me he loved me," says LaRue. LaRue admonished him to be in bed early that night, and Stefano promised he would.

Back at Crawford's, Stefano got ready to attend another meeting of Alcoholics Anonymous. He was planning to hitch a ride with a friend of Murphy's who was scheduled to enter a drug rehab program the next day. They may or may not have attended the meeting. What is known is that, either in lieu of or after doing so, they went to a motel near the corner of Hollywood Boulevard and La Brea Avenue, where they met a dealer named Matt and began doing drugs. After a few hours his companion left, but Stefano stayed behind.

At 11:30 p.m. LaRue called Crawford to check on Stefano. Crawford had to tell him that Stefano wasn't home. He knew it was unlikely that a marathon twelve-step meeting was the reason and put in his nightly call to Kane, who said that Stefano was probably out partying, adding "Don't worry—he always shows up for shoots." Crawford found out where Stefano was at 8 the next morning, when he got a call from Murphy's friend telling him that Stefano was at the motel and that the bill needed to be paid. When he got there Crawford found Stefano slumped in a chair, clearly high but semicoherent. The drug dealer, Matt, still in attendance, supplied the dubious opinion that Stefano was fine, that he was just coming down. Crawford shook Stefano into consciousness, reminding him somewhat pointlessly that he was scheduled to shoot a video in two hours. Clearly, Stefano wouldn't be able to perform, and he nodded his acquiescence when Crawford said he'd call LaRue and tell him Stefano wouldn't be showing up. He also nodded in the affirmative when Crawford asked if he wanted to leave him there to sleep it off. Crawford said he'd be back in a couple of hours and left.

"That was my first mistake," recalls Crawford. But Kane, who had seen Stefano recover from worse states more times than she could remember, also assumed that this was an incident like so many others. They weren't worried; indeed, they spent the next couple of hours shopping for clothes to wear to the upcoming Gay Erotic Video Awards. But when Crawford stopped in at home and told Murphy what had happened, Murphy urged him to get back to the motel. He knew that in the kind of state they'd left Stefano in, with a drug dealer in the room, it was more than likely that he'd keep stoking his system rather than come down.

As soon as he saw Stefano, this time stretched across the bed, his clothes and the bedding soaked with sweat, Crawford knew something was wrong. "His face was almost blue; he didn't look right," Crawford says. "He felt clammy, and I couldn't get a pulse. I screamed at Chris to call 9-1-1 and got him on the ground to give CPR."

Matt again offered the opinion that Stefano would be all right and was opposed to calling an ambulance. "I screamed at Matt, 'Look, if you don't want to get caught, get the fuck out, because we're calling,'" says Crawford. By the time the ambulance arrived, Matt had taken off, and Crawford was trying to revive Stefano with mouth-to-mouth resuscitation. The paramedics took over, and Crawford called Kane a final time. She arrived just as Stefano was being wheeled out on a stretcher. Crawford told the medics that he suspected the drug involved was Special K. They had managed to raise a pulse. Stefano was still technically alive, but they couldn't say whether he'd make it.

They stood for a minute in the motel parking lot, stunned, as the ambulance drove away. "I didn't know how to act," remembers Kane. "It seemed like it was just a drama, a play. Any way that I would've acted would've seemed false. None of my feelings seemed real. I went in and looked at the room he'd been in and thought, *What a horrible place to die.* The bed was damp. There were some wilted roses."

They called LaRue on their way to Cedars-Sinai Medical Center. He closed down the set—where he was filming the scene he was planning to use Joey in—and drove in with another director, John Rutherford, from the studio in the Valley, meeting them in the emergency room. The hospital staff asked for an immediate relative, and Kane supplied Stefano's mother's phone number. But because they weren't relatives, the small group gathered in the hospital waiting room wasn't given any information on Stefano's status, and all sat in numbed, expectant silence. Eventually Kane, anxious and frustrated, told the staff that she was Stefano's fiancée. That seemed to be all the formality needed, and the group was led into another room with a doctor and police officer, where, at about 1 p.m., they were informed Stefano had died. The coroner found a more than deadly combination of drugs in his system: cocaine, morphine, heroin and ketamine (Special K).

They straggled back to Crawford's house, where other friends joined them in an informal mourning session. It was continued later that evening at a restaurant where Gender was performing. Two years previously he'd written new lyrics to the tune of "You Made Me Love You," retitling the song "Dear Mr. Stefano." He sang it for the last time that night, to an audience that included most of Stefano's L.A. friends.

The news of Nick Iacona's death spread quickly. A friend who had known him in Florida and moved to L.A. called Doug

Smith in tears to tell him the news. But no tears came to Smith, who had seen the desperation that had taken hold of Iacona and felt a pang of relief that his troubles, at least, had ended. Smith in turn called Shayo in New York, who was saddened and dismayed that Iacona's self-destruction had finally got the better of him. He got in touch with Iacona's sisters, who were overwhelmed at the expense of transporting the body, not to mention the funeral. Shayo chipped in $1,000 toward expenses, but he couldn't attend the services, planned for the Monday following Iacona's death; he was going out of town on business.

His trip took him through Florida, where he met for lunch with Smith and Trigoura. Smith wanted very much to attend the funeral, though his convenience-store income didn't make it feasible. But Shayo offered to sponsor his trip as well as that of Trigoura. He handed them each $500 for the plane tickets and $100 in spending money. Shayo had not yet met Trigoura, and he was anxious to question him about his relationship with Iacona. But Trigoura, whose reaction to Iacona's death seemed muted, remained largely quiet; he was not a man of many words at the best of times.

Smith and Trigoura took a morning flight from Miami to Philadelphia the Sunday before the funeral. Smith had called Linda and Tina to tell them they would be attending, and Linda had invited them to stay overnight at the house. From Iacona's narration of his family's woes over the years—his talk of sending them money, his proud and diligent supplying of Christmas presents for his nieces and nephew—Smith had formed a picture of the Iacona ménage that was positively Dickensian. "I'd always imagined that I'd walk into a row house and there would be dirt on the floor and children would be running around with no shoes," he recalls. But the picture that presented itself when they caught a cab from the airport late Sunday afternoon was far less humble and less dramatic. The house lacked none of the charms associated with middle-class respectability, though some of them were familiar to Smith, who recognized them as Iacona's things that he'd shipped from Florida. The children were well-behaved and well-groomed. The family had just passed a sad Thanksgiving, but there were leftovers in abundance, and Smith, Trigoura, and the family sat down to a buffet dinner.

Linda and Tina performed hosting duties. Although Iacona's mother was present, Smith had been struck by her anguish from the moment they walked in: She sat stonily staring at a television set throughout the evening, quietly acknowledging their introduction without withdrawing from her sad reverie. As Linda and Tina had quietly explained to the two men, Helen Iacona, a simple and deeply religious woman, had never been apprised of the sources of her son's income. Nor had she been aware of the depth of his difficulties with drugs. So his death, which was hardly shocking to those who had watched his struggles over the years, naturally came as a violent upheaval to his mother, who had been carefully shielded from knowledge of his most desperate straits.

After dinner Mrs. Iacona and the children went to bed, and Smith, Trigoura, and Iacona's sisters assembled upstairs in Linda's room, where they sat talking into the night. The two men had swiped an ample supply of alcohol from the airplane on the way in, and they mixed what was at hand. Smith was curious about Iacona's childhood, and Tina recalled Iacona's dancing for the family as a little boy to various disco songs. He'd always had the instincts of a performer. They talked about his affection for the kids, whom he'd treat to candy whenever possible and to a crisp dollar bill when they'd pull on his leg. And despite the sad circumstance of his death, they talked about the wilder times they'd shared with Iacona, who had been the supplier of intoxicants as well as candy to his family and friends, even on their most recent trip to the shore; it was a subject that seemed to upset only Trigoura.

Smith and Trigoura slept on Stefano's feather mattress that night, waking early the next morning. Trigoura wanted to pick up a camera to take pictures of the house and family, so they set off early, taking the kids with them and treating them to candy and breakfast while Linda and Tina prepared for the funeral. When they returned, all climbed into a limousine for the short ride to the Ward Funeral Home in nearby Linwood. Smith and Trigoura more or less kept to themselves at the service, observing Iacona's family and hometown friends from a distance. Despite Iacona's spectacularly public face in the gay world, his career and the notoriety it brought him had largely not penetrated the insulated world of suburban Philly. The laminated obituary notice handed out at the service referred obliquely to his career: "He was employed as a model with several agencies for the last six years." And Smith didn't think it was the time to illuminate anyone on the successes of Iacona's alter ego, Joey Stefano. "I didn't talk to anybody or introduce myself because I didn't feel like answering a bunch of questions," he remembers. "And how were we going to introduce Alain to these people?" It wasn't clear whether the twenty to thirty family members and friends in attendance even had an inkling that Iacona was gay. The mourners included a veritable battalion of nuns in full habit, friends of Iacona's mother.

The young man who had lived a life on the more exotic fringes of gay society was laid to rest at home in traditional style; there wasn't a drag queen in sight as a priest gave a short reading before the open casket. The guests filed by to pay their last respects or kneel before the casket for a prayer. Smith looked at Iacona's lifeless face with numb disbelief. It wasn't the face he knew, the face that was on display in the photographs from Iacona's legit modeling portfolio that Linda had displayed on the casket. Trigoura impulsively snapped a photograph as he passed in front of the bier. It was fitting that the mechanical device that had given Nick Iacona so much, and perhaps taken away more, should have a last snatch at his image.

The procession moved through the gray gloom of a drizzly Philadelphia fall day to the Immaculate Heart Cemetery, where Iacona would be buried next to his father. The earth was wet and the rain picked up as the short interment ceremony was read. "It was a perfect day for a burial," Smith remembers. He and Trigoura were among the six pallbearers, and they returned to Linda's house with the family afterward to receive family and friends stopping by with food. But Smith felt oppressed by a strange sense that the part of Iacona's life that he had known had to be kept secret here, that in some fashion he was attending the funeral of a man entirely other than the one who had been his friend for the past five years. He and Trigoura were both anxious to get back to Florida, where they wouldn't feel that the Nick Iacona they had known, the man who had made a career of his spectacular gay sexuality, was a source of shame, that his odyssey was an unspeakable perversion of the life of the nice Catholic boy they'd just seen laid to rest.

That Iacona's sisters had shared with some of the family friends at least the rough outlines of his unconventional career only became apparent to Smith and Trigoura as they rode to the airport. A couple of friends of the family offered to take them by some of the sites of Iacona's youth on the way, and they saw a glimpse of his high school as well as the apartment he had grown up in in Chester, now in a neighborhood that had deteriorated considerably since his family had moved away. Their hosts asked Smith and Trigoura if they too were in the porn industry and peppered them with questions about stars. But that they were curious about *female* stars indicated either a naïveté about the general segregation between the straight and gay video worlds or the idea that they believed Joey Stefano had been a star of straight video. Smith side-stepped the questions as best he could, not wanting to shed any more light than necessary. Nor did he chime in when talk turned to the ample and high-quality drugs Iacona had supplied—sadly, this appeared to be the chief common ground between Iacona's porn lifestyle and his hometown milieu, the grim thread that knitted together all the corners of his life and finally tore it apart.

His death was ruled accidental, and it will probably never be known if his overdose was a willed act of suicide. Like so many of his deepest griefs, whose sources he hid from even his close friends, as if they were things to be ashamed of, his state of mind in his last hours was something he kept to himself. As if to make up for the squandering of his physical presence, his body that was on constant public display and available by the hour, Nick Iacona fiercely guarded his deepest feelings.

What he hadn't been able to hide was a terrible hunger for oblivion, a desire to escape the world as often as possible and for as long as possible. It was the hunger that drove him to drugs—the one constant in both his Philadelphia home and the various ports of call he briefly stopped in—and that burned behind his exhaustive pursuit of the ecstasy of sex. For Nick Iacona, in the end, it was a hunger stronger than the human instinct for life; it was a need that could be satisfied only in death.

VIDEOGRAPHY

This is a listing of some of Stefano's more notable and widely available videos. But gay porn has a relatively short shelf life, so many if not most will not be available at your average video store. The Catalina and Falcon titles are perhaps easiest to find.

Big Bang (Falcon, 1990). Stefano's best video for Falcon, in which he's teamed with Michael Parks and plays against type, as it were, dominating Parks throughout, even when he's getting fucked. He also tops Parks and is obviously having a great time being on the giving end. The scene seems more spontaneous than usual, unlike most videos, in which you can almost hear the director giving instructions to change position. The video's cover stars, Mark Baxter and Glenn Steers, also have a great scene. More familiar faces from Stefano's video history—Lon Flexx, Matt Gunther, and Chris Stone—are also featured in a four-way finale with the presumably French Luc Francois.

Bi-Golly (Bi-Line Productions, 1993). Karen Dior was the uncredited director on this cheapie bisexual video, in which Stefano gives one of his most disaffected performances. To call it a performance is generous, in fact. He scowls throughout, and watching his partner attempt to enter him with a dildo is like watching someone struggling to open a door with the wrong key. But he looks perhaps more gorgeous than ever—with long, sculpted sideburns and his hair in a full pompadour. The other scenes, all of which take place on a kitschy Western set featuring such accoutrements as a bale of hay (where do you find one of those in the Valley?) and a bag of horse feed, are better.

Billboard (Catalina, 1989). Chi Chi LaRue's first bigger-budget feature with Stefano is one of their best collaborations. Stefano, who is top-billed, is featured in three scenes, the first two with rather plastic costars Adam Grant and Vic Summers. The best comes last, a three-way with frequent partner Lon Flexx and Chris Stone. The painting-studio plot is minimal but not insulting, and the sex scenes are polished and engaging. With Andrew Michaels, Dusty, and Chris Ramsey.

Buddy System II (Vivid Video, 1989). The first video Stefano filmed, though you'd never guess it from his sexual aplomb. His first scene features Gino Colbert as an abusive sergeant, with Stefano the surly but obedient recruit. It's unspectacular. But the finale, with fellow LaRue fixtures Ryan Yeager and the lush-lipped Andrew Michaels, is one of his best scenes, bar none. He's in a sling, with Michaels and Yeager taking turns at either end. In that scene and in a duo with Tony Davis, Yeager displays the aggressive sexiness—despite unspectacular looks—that made him the yin to Stefano's yang, the top who was the biggest find of LaRue's early career.

Fond Focus (In-Hand, 1989). An early LaRue low-budgeter that shows Stefano off to good effect, if nothing else. A three-way with Steve Kennedy and Alex Stone on an outdoor tennis court, of all places, is the highlight. The plot concerns Stefano and his stepfather's growing intimacy, but the guy playing his stepfather is rather icky, particularly compared to the guys on the tennis court, so the climax, when they fall into each other's arms, is disappointing.

Hard Knocks (In-Hand, 1990). An early LaRue production distinguished primarily by its finale, in which the spooky Jon Vincent has his way with a roomful of boys, including Stefano, Tony Davis, Andrew Michaels, and Domino. Vincent, beefy and with a mean leer on his face, obviously improvises his dialogue, ordering people to service him willy-nilly ("Hey! Everybody get off the couch!"). The entire thing takes place on a giant sheet of black plastic with naked boys strewn around it, like an under-budgeted Versace ad come to libidinous life.

Hard Steal (Catalina, 1989). A high-budget John Travis production, one of Stefano's more polished films, with a jewel-thief plotline that provides the occasion for the requisite bad acting. The blond, beefy Rod Phillips and Stefano have an extended scene that benefits from the fact that they were dating each other at the time. The rest of the cast is fairly generic but top of the line nonetheless.

Idol Eyes (Matt Sterling, 1990). Minimal plotting, and what there is is dopey, but the sex scenes are exquisitely rendered, full of beautiful, coiffed creatures glistening under perfect studio lighting. The cast is top-notch, with Idol making his debut, and includes Matt Gunther and Chris Stone. Idol's one sex scene is with Stefano, and it's one of Stefano's best. He seems inspired by Idol's bruised Ken-doll beauty and ample endowment. They make an astonishingly beautiful pair.

More of a Man (All Worlds, 1991). Indisputably among Stefano's best films and certainly the most sophisticated, plot-wise. Stefano plays a construction worker in the process of coming out and falling in love. Chi Chi LaRue is his drag queen confidant. Michael Henson is the love interest. It also contains Stefano's only teaming with sizable legend Rick Donovan, though the scene doesn't show off either at their best. But Stefano's scene with Henson is excellent. There's also an incendiary orgy scene, and LaRue gets a big musical number.

Plunge (Falcon, 1990). A generic if fairly polished Falcon title, meaning the men are all well-groomed, attractive, and professionally up to par. Stefano has an extended Jacuzzi scene with Lon Flexx (who doesn't wear a condom). Probably the least interesting of Stefano's three Falcon videos.

Prince Charming (Vivid Video, 1991). This camp send-up of medieval kitsch is a lot of fun and features great sex. Brian Yates plays the prince, who stumbles into a few beds, including stable boy Stefano's, in his search for true love. Sets are amusingly cheesy, and the acting matches. Stefano's scene with Yates is odd for him; he plays nasty and tosses Yates about a little, though he spends most of the time rimming him. An uncut version is apparently very scandalous, though hard to find. The cast makes up in enthusiasm what it lacks in star quality.

Revenge: More Than I Can Take (Falcon, 1990). What the title has to do with this plotless video is anyone's guess. A bunch of guys show up at a hotel, with pool, and have sex. Stefano is teamed with Jon Vincent in a good if unspectacular scene. Vincent's scene with the pretty brunet going by the name of Domino is rather better. Also with Michael Parks, Luke Bender, and Steve Kreig.

Scoring (Vivid Video, 1991). Jim Steel and Chi Chi LaRue conceived and directed this middling fare, distinguished primarily by Stefano's finale scene with newcomer Steve Ryder, long-haired and beefy. They go at it in a pool of light in the middle of darkness, which heightens the drama. The rest of the video is standard cheapo sex.

Sex in Wet Places (Catalina, 1992). Directed by Chi Chi LaRue (as Taylor Hudson), *Wet Places* is a sort of sequel to the more inventive *Sex in Tight Places,* which features boys going at it in various confined environments (a phone booth, an elevator). The scenes in *Wet Places* all take place in or near water. The blond box-cover boy Bo Summers, taking a very long bath, fantasizes about various couplings: Wes Daniels and Brett Ford by a pool (with sunglasses throughout); the boyish brunet Randy Mixer with Summers in a waterfall. Stefano's partner is Kurt Manning, a somewhat stocky performer with a sexy, muttlike face. Stefano is near his prime here and enthusiastically gets reamed on a weight bench. The momentum of the scene, unfortunately, is diminished by LaRue's arty cutting in of bits from other scenes.

Sex, lies and videocassettes (Sierra Pacific, 1989). A plot-driven video in which Stefano plays a young model wanna-be who comes to L.A. under the tutelage of a leering queen who promises him *GQ* layouts but delivers him to prostitution and disappointment. Contrasted with this is the sweet story of Jared Young, who finds happiness in the gay-porn biz. It's quaintly simplistic propaganda for the porn biz, which, considering the audience it's reaching, amounts to preaching to the choir. Stefano has one of his best scenes with frequent partner Lon Flexx, and the on-the-set porn sequences give an approximation of the milieu. With Bill Marlowe, John Fell, and Chris McKenzie.

Songs in the Key of Sex (HIS Video, 1992). One of Chi Chi LaRue's more elaborate extravaganzas, this saga of an up-and-comer in the music biz, played by Randy Mixer, would be a little more persuasive if Mixer could carry a tune. Or act. Oh, well, he's cute and a good sexual performer. Stefano has a supporting role—or rather, scene—in which he's paired with

Wes Daniels and gets fucked wildly. Also with Jason Ross, Chance Caldwell, Brett Ford, and Sharon Kane as a nightclub chanteuse with a closetful of wigs.

Tijuana Toilet Tramps (Stallion Video, 1994). One of Stefano's last films, this pseudo documentary has a camp edge that makes it endearing. Purporting to witness the nasty goings-on at a tearoom, the video features occasional man-on-the-toilet interviews conducted by an offscreen Gino Colbert. So Chip Daniels is interrupted while working Miguel Lopez's cock with the question "'Scuze me, sir, can you tell me what you're doing?" The boyish Daniels, with a chipper grin, replies, "Sure, I'm sucking a cock right now that's really juicy!" Stefano's scene with the balding, beefy Anthony Gallo kicks off the video. His long hair is pulled back in a ponytail, and his body is buffed. He seems to be having a pretty good time too, but there's a notable roteness to his behavior.